NOTES
ON THE PAST
IMPERFECT

SEAN WALSH

About Sean Walsh:

I've worked and lived in communications all my life: journalist, subeditor, editor, actor, director, producer - here in Ireland and abroad.

I fell in love with Hiberno-English a long time ago - English as it is spoken and written in my country - and have been in love with it ever since.

I love the wind and the sea and the mountains, fresh air and green grass and the sun on my back (I play a mean game of golf) - all of which I have around me here in Dublin, Ireland.

Not to mention the warm humour that wells up from a big heart.

If I may share with you some of the gems that have influenced me down the years; I try to abide by them but don't always succeed!

"You make your way by taking it...

"It does not just happen, you have to make it happen...

"Sometimes in stooping down to pick up two pennies one can lose a fortune..."

Interests:

Friendship - when it is not possessive, controlling...

Quiet. Silence. A positive value completely overlooked by many today...

Reading - carefully judged. If I'm not hooked by the first sequence I won't read any further...

—

Trying, day in day out, not to spill any more milk... and to stop crying over milk already spilt.

Not suffering fools gladly...

Analysing Casablanca, frame for frame, line by line...

Publications:
My scripts have been broadcast on RTE, Radio One, BBC 4 and, in translation, on European networks; televised on RTE One, BBC One and Channel 4; staged at the Peacock by the Abbey National Theatre, at the Project, the Eblana, the Liverpool Playhouse and on the London Fringe...

Credits include *The Night of the Rouser.*
Earwig.
The Dreamers.
Fugitive.
Veil.
Penny for Your Travels.
Far Side of the Moon.
Three for Calvary.
Jenny One, Two, Three...
The Circus.
Centre Circle.
Where Do We Go from Here, My Lovely?
Pilate Under Pressure.
Conclave.
Assault on a Citadel.

I have facilitated many workshops on Creative/Script Writing in Dublin and at various centres around Ireland.

Favourite authors:
A D Sertillanges. John Henry Newman. Waugh. Greene.
Hemingway. Hans Kung.

Films I cherish:
Ben Hur. A Man for all Seasons. Jesus of Montreal. Of Gods
and Men.

Likes:
Good conversation. The company of my fellow searchers...

Dislikes:
Arrogant, self-opinionated prigs... Controlling, bullying
clerics...

Favourite Quotes:
"I passionately hate the idea of being with it. I think an artist
has always to be out of step with his time." (Orson Welles
(1915 - 1985)

"Sometimes you have to go on when you don't feel like it,
and sometimes you're doing good work
when it feels like all you're managing is to shovel
shit from a sitting position."
- Stephen King
On Writing: A Memoir of the Craft.

—

About this book:

Not easy to define - literary fiction, a kind of memoir, more than somewhat autobiographical...

A mosaic of sorts. Irish Voices from the past... Spiced with a wry sense of humour.

Writing "within myself"- for sure...

'Will make you forget you are reading a book..? Again, for sure.

I write, speak, hear Hiberno-English...

I avoid the traditional narrative format for the most part; I prefer direct speech - monologue, dialogue. (I've left out the bits the readers would skip, anyway!)

To begin to read... then find yourself listening... to a voice, voices... from another place, another time...

Voices from Ireland of the 80's... (Before Civil Divorce became law in the Irish Republic.) Phone calls, recalls, spilt milk... The pain and the laughter, sorrow and joy, of a yesterday world.

My favourite format? Radio Drama. By far. At its very best the listener is a fly-on-the-wall: eavesdropping, over-hearing, listening in, privy to the most intimate, soul-searching monologue, revealing dialogue...

I worked in RTE's Drama Department for some 16 years in the '70's,'80's - directing, producing, scripting, editing.

During that period I wrote and produced some of my own plays; well received and reviewed for the most part, they were subsequently broadcast by the BBC and, in translation, on many European networks.

If my writing shows a heavy influence dating back to that time, well, I make no apology for that.

Later... some years into my (early) retirement... it began to occur to me: six of my scripts were inter-related, in the same mould/vein, out of the same stable, so to speak... similar, complementary story-lines...

So, Sean, re-work them as chapters/sections/ in print format and hey, you have yourself a book!

The storyline moves forward and back - sometimes sideways! Disjointed narrative - rather than neatly strung together...

At times I knew where I was going - or so I thought. At other times I was drawing a chain out of muddy water - a link at a time.

Kept putting it aside, it kept re-surfacing, demanding an audience, readership.

This to give you an idea of what I'm at, where I'm coming from...

Warning!
If your need is to be spoon-fed, if you have little desire to be challenged, mentally stimulated, if you wish to be left undisturbed in your comfort zone... then NOTES ON THE PAST IMPERFECT is not for you!

CONTENTS

Book Three
Dead Man Talking
Shock. Aftershock. Wave after wave... As he comes to
realise that his wife has gone, gone for good, he begins
to talk - to himself, to his nine-years-old daughter, to a
"local in his local," to a parish sage, to a solicitor, to his
Boss at work, to clerics, to a psychiatrist...

Book Four
Penny for Your Travels
The session with the psychiatrist at the close of the
previous chapter leads to: Scenes from an Irish
boyhood. Not so much Voyage round my Father as
Travels with my Dad... A man looks back at his
formative years, early adolescence... Snatches from the
past... fragments from a world long forgotten... A kind
of mosaic rather than a formal memoir

Book Five
Playback
Evening. He gets home, checks his voice mail as is his
wont... listens, bemused, to various recorded
messages... tenses, frowns as he hears a far-away voice
from a distant past: his estranged wife speaking to,
pleading with, her daughter, Jenny, now well into her
teens... And so begins a chain reaction...

Book Six
Jenny One, Two, Three

—

Dad in Dublin takes a call from daughter in London triggering in him a chain reaction: he recalls her childhood, adolescence, early womanhood... their relationship over the years. A love story, then, of a different kind. Dad Jenny. Any Dad, any daughter. Any where, any time... *"But for all our rows and fallings-out, I love you, Dad. 'No matter what. And always will..."*

READERS' COMMENTS:

"A cascade of words which seems to tumble out one on top of the other before disappearing in any number of poetic eddies. Brings to mind reading Francoise Segan…"
                    - Bro J.

"The tears are flowing freely. This writer can put things into words that I can only feel - so much of this book is flaying me that I don't have any words right now. I'm hurting, but it's a hurt that I can deal with and I value."
                    - J O S.

"The piece is quite marvellous. Maybe that's what great lit does for us - allows us to recognise our own loving selves, and to weep the tears we have been holding captive to prevent them unmanning us. I can't think of anything that gets so close to the dear places I too have been to."
                    - S O'C.

"I read this haunting piece - not knowing what to expect - totally gripped. Wow is about the best I can muster for now... so hit by the rawness and swept away by the fluidity..."
                    - J.W.

"It was moving and tender… A deep, soft poignancy that's really touching, enclosing, quietly rhythmic…"
                    - G. P.

"Riveting. It's like looking at a mirror obscured by condensation, and making out the detail just a bit at a time from a developing mosaic of clues…"
                    - S O'C.

CENTRE CIRCLE

Hello, Pat?.. Eh no, I'm back - just in the door this minute...
And am I glad to be home?!.. 'Wouldn't wish it on my worst
enemy... Rough?!.. As a badger's arse – if you'll excuse the
expression.

Oh, I knew it wasn't going to be a picnic but God Almighty!..
'Had to sit there, listen to some of the staff having a go...
'Felt sorry for her in a way, to be honest...
And it's cold turkey. If you're caught nibbling, you're out...

Oh, I did, yes. I, I said a few – words...
Well, so far so good - touch wood. Oh, she seems to be taking
it on the chin, anything they throw at her...
Better able to handle it than I was, I can tell you...

Ah, I think myself they overdo it –
'go for the juggler every time... Still, if it gets results...
They say three weeks, they'll see after that...

Could be the makings of her - if she goes the distance...
Ah, please God... This time, this time... We won't know
ourselves...

What - sorry?.. Oh, yeah. Better. Bound to be.
Maybe not any easier - but better...

Oh, I know that, Patricia... You're a real friend
and a great neighbour - one of the best...
Ah, come on now! Not everyone would...
Most of them round here don't want to know -
not that I blame them...

Anyway, how is the wee one?.. Ah, that's...
No, no if she's playing with Deirdre, leave her be...
I'll be over to pick her up as soon as I -
No - no the weekend's no problem. She'll be fine, I'll
manage...

So I suppose himself will be in the door any minute?..
Ah now, he's A One in my book... Oh, I will, sure. 'Love to...

One of these nights himself and myself will go out for a few -
eh, when I'm a bit better organized... All right, then...
See you soon... Bye for now... Bye, Pat...

Hmmmm... Must get her something - voucher, token...
'Bottle of wine, maybe, from the off-license...

I didn't tell her the half of it. Patricia. Maybe never will.
'Tell her how it really went... 'Not easy to admit to yourself,
never mind to another...

And I didn't give them the full story either, did I? No. No, I
didn't... Not with her there, taking it in... The lip curled in a
half-smile as she watched me - squirm...

Shit! Oh, shit!.. What a day. What a bloody awful day...
'Should have seen it coming... 'Took my eye off the ball...

'Could kick myself. And her... Emma. Dear, dearest Emma.
My wayward wife... 'Kick her from here to - Ah, if ever
there was a maverick!..
'Never forget this day - not if I live to be ninty!

———

'Long walk down a short corridor - into a roomful of strangers… Emma across from me - strangest of them all… And how was I to know - how was I to know! - that the spotlight would turn on me?..

Wh-what?.. Me?.. Oh-hh... Well, I, I... God...
I, I'm here because my, my wife there is, is…
So I want to, to help if, if I can... as much as I...
And our wee one. She doesn't deserve...
Anything to, to sort out this, this mess,
get back to, to where we were...

When one of you - I'm not sure who -
anyway, one of the C-Counselors here -
rang me at work - asking me to, to participate -
it was the last thing I wanted to do, I can tell you!
But she said something about a, a family illness.
That gave me a gunk for a start. 'Didn't see it like that. Not
at all...

Oh, I know - 'know for a good while now - that she...
that my - that Emma has a, a problem - as they say.
But I didn't want to know - if, if you know what I mean.

What?.. Oh, yes. We did. 'Did drink together.
At first. In the beginning. In, in the old days...
Some good times, 'won't deny that... And she,
she could hold her own in any company.
At first... At first.

Ah-hh-hhh... 'Got out of hand... Messing. Rows - arguments...
Repetitious bullshit... Always ended the same... Em-
embarrassing... So I, eh, I began to - disengage. Let her off...

Well, no... I enjoy a drink, I don't mind telling you.
The company, the craic, the lads. Ah, mighty!
They know my form - end of story. God,
if I didn't show they'd send out a search party!

Sorry?.. Well, yes, mostly... It's a good local.
They keep a tight rein, no messers...
'Look after their regulars... 'Not far, there and back -
and sure the car knows its own way by now! Ha, ha.

Hmmm?.. Ah, just the few of us. Evenings, mostly.
It was a round but you always knew where you stood.
'Never got out of hand... And, and if it went on a bit,
there was always the slate...

Oh, weekends, yes... And, and... No, not every night...
Yes... Well, yes... Almost every... Oh, all right, then!
Every bloody night - if it makes you - !

Two, three pints - maybe a chaser –
so what's wrong with that?!

What was that?.. No. No, not with anyone!
By no means... no. Always careful who I...
'Proud to he seen with them, they with me...
All, all quite successful in their own way...

Well… now and then... maybe...
if they were gone home... or, or didn't show...
or there wasn't much doing...
I, I'd talk to the barman or...
or whoever happened to be...
No - no matter who...

What?.. No, never. The job always came first.

If I was dying with a hangover I'd still make it -

and on time!.. Hmmm?.. Well, once... maybe twice...

I, I got her to ring in, say I had a bad back or -

But they were isolated, very isolated - !..

I, I'd say I performed as, as well as the next man...

Eh-hh... I, I suppose, yes... Yes, I...

It, it would be nearer the mark...

to say... to admit... that my work suffered...

over the years... as a result... of my...

Look, who's being treated here - her or me?!..

No, I'm not getting edgy!..

It's just that - !.. I am relaxed!..

Sorry?.. Well, no... But I'm sure

if I really put my mind to it, I'd he able to, to...

Well, one year, yes. For - for Lent...

No, not quite. I broke down - I mean, I broke out...

Visitors or something - I forget.

Or maybe I just got fed up drinking Orange - standing on the
pier while the rest of the lads drifted out to sea...

Oh, I know what you're saying, what you're getting at!
But I'm telling you, if I once made up my mind to quit,
I'd quit. No problem... Sure, how many of my mates
have told me - assured me - that I don't have a, a..?
No way. And if they didn't know, who would?!..

Look, if you're trying to mark my card,
you're going the wrong way about it...
I'm no saint but I kept my job
and the roof over our heads
and the bread on the table and... and...

Huh?.. That's right, the bills, 'paid the - hmmm?..
Well, to be honest with you, I'd nearly always leave it to
the... Oh... What are you - a mind reader?..

Yes, as a matter of fact -
but it was only the once, an isolated case!..
I just forgot to... Eh-hh, twice at the most...

El-electricity... They came to cut us off.

Well, the amount - plus a re-connection fee...

Look, all that means is I'm human - right?

'Not much different from the next man...

Hmmm?.. Well, yes - especially at the, at the weekends...

'Party here, a do there... Someone would give me the beck

and I'd get a few half-dozens - or a bottle of white, litre of

red.

Ah, it'd go on - you can imagine - into the small hours.

What?.. Well - dancing... Sorry?..

'Messed, yes. Yes, messed... C-Close dancing...

With that sort of music and low eh, soft lights...

But I never - that's as far as it went... I mean, mooching...

and, and kissing... and necking... But that's as far... far as...

And, and sometimes her husband wouldn't be that far away

and he'd be hard at it, too - mooching and, and necking and

kissing - eh, usually with another bird. Ha, ha - sorry...

But no, never... Not once... ever...
That's as far as it went... Ever...
Far as I'd go... Ever... Never... Not once...
I never... ever... did...

Sorry, I - ?.. How do y'mean, change?..
Sure, l wouldn't he drinking the stuff
if it didn't have some effect on me,
the price of it!

Well... at first I might be tired, a bit shagged,
and after a while it would give me a lift
and I'd be as right as rain...

When - when I got home?.. Well, if -
if things weren't right,
na-naturally I'd get annoyed...
Well, wouldn't anyone?.. Hmmm?..

Like if there was no dinner... or sign of herself.
The milk bottle, maybe, still on the door-step.
The post in the hall.
A bill jumping up to bite me in the neck.

A dead fire in the grate.
'Pile of dishes in the sink.
'Sea of fluff on the carpet.
No sign of the house-keeping money
that was supposed to last the week –
not to mention the children's allowance!

Wee things like that... Yeah, I'd get annoyed... A bit.
Are you joking me?.. I'd bloodywell throw the head!

What?.. Yes. Yes, I agree... 'Course I'd have to agree...
Mood, change of mood, my mood would have changed...

So?.. Look, I'll give you ten to one the only man in my shoes
who wouldn't change would be the Man in the Moon!..
And the same odds that herself there -
if he was hitched to her - would wipe the smile off even his
face!..

De-demanding?.. I, I suppose you could say that.
I, I wanted everything to be - right...
I might be out of order but I wanted
everyone and everything around me
to be in order - if, if you know what I mean...

Tense, yeah. Uptight... 'Not knowing
if she'd be in or out, or what way she'd be.
Maybe even away - no note, nothing.
'Wait and wonder, see if she'd show...
condescend to put in an appearance.

And if she was in, it could be up in the sack,
sleeping it off...
Or in an armchair, the sun glasses on,
nursing a glass of plonk, gawking at TV...
Talk about Fawlty Towers? Jesus!..

Or one of them cookery programmes...
Oh, a dab hand at watching someone else
doing Medallions of Beef Chasseur.
The grin on her when it came to the wine sauce -
like a cat after cream...

Ah, you can imagine. 'Only took a spark!..
I'd say something, she'd hit back.
She'd bounce a ball, I'd kick it.
Never wanted for a sparring partner
as long as she was around...

Are you hungry, luv? Well, you know
where the kitchen is.
There's feck-all in the fridge
but help yourself to the linoleum:
the lump that's sticking up in the corner,
if you chaw it off, I'd be grateful...

Eh-hh?.. Just the one. Jenny... Nine... Ah-hh...
There was a time you couldn't shut her up.
Now?.. 'Hard to get a word out of her.
'Gone in on herself a lot.
Sullen, you might say. Resentful...

Her school reports are dire...
And when she gets stuck into the telly
you'd think, be God, it was the Taj Mahal
she were sitting in front of!..

My, my job?.. Ah-hh... Not great, to be honest.
The daggers are out. I can sense, feel it...
In the office, the Department.
A hint here, an innuendo there...
Jealousy. Oh, no doubt.

And my Boss?!.. No matter what I do, it doesn't
seem to satisfy him... 'Always finding fault.
Ah, such moods!.. 'Wouldn't surprise me if he had a problem
- with the drink, like... 'Bloody bully, that's all he is...

What's that?.. Why, yes, as a matter of fact...
'Few years ago.. The job was boarded.
I did a very good interview - I know I did.
Ah, what I wasn't gonna do!
But they gave it to your man - Golden Boy...
Well, they lived to rue the day, I can tell you!..
Hmmm?.. 'Course I should have got it! Sure I should!

Maybe a bit of back-up from herself there -
some support - would have made a difference!
All the difference in the world, if you ask me...

What? Sorry?.. Blame?.. Well, yes, of course.
'Course I blame her! Only for her I - !..
Well, I wouldn't he here for one thing!
Home, that's where I'd be! With my family.
Or out, out with the lads... Normal...

Huh?.. No. No, I'm not blameless. Certainly not!..
No, I never said I... Look, all I'm trying to... What?..
I, I come across as, as blaming it all on -
'Blame everyone - everything - except, 'cept myself?..

How do you mean, de-deflecting?.. A-attention...
away from, from myself?.. Tran-transfer of guilt?..
Ah well, if you're going to drown me in jargon,
smother me with cliches, blind me with platitudes!

You know it all and I know fuck-all...
I tell it like it is and you
throw it back at me!
Well, sorry, but that seems to be
where you're coming from...

Look, you can talk away at me
till the cows come home
but I know my own know -
and I'll tell you this for nothing:
only for her I wouldn't be
up to my neck in shit!..

I, I was wondering when you'd ask me that...
Eh-hh, yes... I'd have to say - that, too...
'Hate to admit... 'Hate myself for...
Looking back now... God. God forgive me.
'No excuse - or maybe reason enough, I dunno...
Yes, I do, too - I do know!..

Look, I - I am what I am...
as I am... right here and now...
Would you say I was a, a storm trooper?..
'Strike you as a sadist?.. I wouldn't hurt a...
Honest. Honest to God...
But I can be, can be pushed - provoked...
You can take so much and then, then -
something snaps and you, you hit out...

'With me, anyway. I do, I did... B-belted her, yes.
A, a swing... push... in rage... seething.
She'd say to me - taunting – 'Look at your face'
Look at my face?!
How the Hell could I look in the mirror
without taking my eye off her, dropping my guard?..

No, of course not. Of course you don't hit a woman.
I'll go along with that. Certainly. All the way...
But, but suppose you really come up against it?
Huh?.. What about that?.. Stand there and take it -
take all she can throw at you - is that it?..

'Packs a punch, I can tell you...
'Clawed, scratched, scrabbed... Oh, aye!..
My glasses snatched, twisted - maybe broken...
Her hands at my throat, on my windpipe...
'Kneed in the groin, the goolies... Yes! Oh, yes!..

What, for God's sake! What do you expect of me?
Chivalry - or self-defence?..
And when I broke free... re-retaliated...
she threw herself, screaming, to the floor...
and Jenny - terrified, petrified Jenny -
shot out of a warm, tucked-in, bed -
launched herself from a rainbow dream -
down the stairs and into a chaotic kitchen
to seize up the situation at a glance
and accuse me - me! -
of, of maltreating her mother...

And still does, I suspect... I know.
To this day... somewhere, somehow...
deep in her subconscious...
there is the gnawing suspicion -
malignant cancer -
that I - I... savaged her Mummy...

You have no idea - how could you? -
how alien all that is to, to me..
I mean, I know a fair number
of women and honest to God -
ladies and gentlemen - father, fathers -
if there's a reverend among you -
it would take a lot, an awful lot,
for any one of them to, to
raise my hackles... that, that much...

It would have to be, be something very much
out of the or-ordinary... Ordinary... Out of the...
I suppose, what I'm trying to say is when,
when she was jarred and we, we met, head-on...
and I was jarred... I - I was less of a man...
and she, she was dif-different...

Yeah, I think so. That, that would be it. I reckon, yes.

Weaker sex? She frightens the Hell out of me!

A landmine in the front room would be safer...

At least I could do something about that -

call in the army, have it diffused...

You can do that - with a bomb...

But she - she is something else...

Herself there... 'Good person in ways.

Good turn in her. 'Wants so much to be a good mother...

But give her the smell of a cork, then try to reason with her?..

You might as well be talking to the wall...

So... Can we please leave it at that?

For now, anyway... How do I feel?..

Well, to be honest - I, I'm out of the game...

What?.. Sorry?!.. Am I hearing you?..

You reckon I, too, have a, a... Me?..

I, I'd make very good ma-material?..

You, you want me to do, do the course?..

The two of us - together?..

You'd expect to make real progress?..

Jesus... Wha'!..

Look, I... It, it's not as easy as that.
Even if I was willing to, to...
There's the house and my job
and I, I'd have to dream up a story,
get someone to cover for me.
And the wee one would need to be -

What?.. Yes, I know, 'know the house
will still be standing when I - I'm not an idiot...
I suppose, yes. Yes, I dare say I'd be able to function better -
do a better day's work - 'make up for...

Huh?.. You're joking, of course!.. Jenny..?!
You, you want me to bring her here? Here?!..
For a, a session or two?.. Participate?..
My child - to this, this Centre?!
Have her sit in on a, a -
among a circle of strangers?!
'Watch and listen while they
shovel shit at each other?!

You must be out of your skull!!..
For, for Emma's sake?.. And, and mine?..

Well, what about for Jenny's sake?! Huh!?..
Look, I'll ring you - okay?..

How dare they! How fucking dare they!..
Counselors?! Sadists, the lot of them!..
No sympathy. No milk of human kindness...

Still... 'Come to think of it... That's how they...
Well skilled in dealing with the devious...
Maybe, maybe that's why they had a go at me - so they
could get at her.

And she fell for it, into the trap...
Yes. Yes, that's the way it was, I reckon.
Why they drew me in the first place - into the net.
To set me up - so they could set her up...

—

And when I began, dry-mouthed -

faltering, fumbling, searching for words -

eyes to the floor, the far wall,

not knowing what to say,

where to -

she spat across the room -

Look at me when you're speaking!

You could hear a pin drop...

They saw it on her face, in her eyes,

heard it in her voice: hard, demanding...

coldly impervious.

It was the "in" they had been waiting for.

By God, they gave her a roasting!

You're a bitch, Emma!..

You've been verbally castrating your husband for years!..

A drug addict chipped in:

Takes one to know one...

And from another angle, another Counselor -

Emma, you're full of shit!..

I looked away as she fought back the tears.
She was, after all, my, my - no matter what…
And then, recovery: tilt of the head,
shake of the hair as she rallied, defiant.
No way were they going to break her.
Not by a long chalk...

I was in bits leaving. At Reception,
she was suddenly at my side, forlorn:

Don't feel sorry for me. I brought it on myself...

Then she turned and went, went back in...

But will she stay the pace, go the distance?..
No follow-through. Ever. 'Starts something -
sudden burst of enthusiasm - then loses interest...
Or as soon as she runs into bad weather -
a rough patch - backs off, bails out, drops it...

—

Maybe drops us all in it...

But this time… something about her...

I'd nearly think that maybe... just maybe...

Well, after all, she went in of her own…

Hugh, eh?.. Hughie.

God, if ever there was a hard man!

Many's the session we had in the old days -

Oh, what! 'Gave it a lash!..

No one ever thought he'd go on the dry,

make it to the other side of the street.

'Few years ago now... Christmas Eve.

Hugh holding on to the bar, langers.

'Calls for a double, lets it back, passes out...

'Woke the next day - or was it the day after? -

in the Quare Place...

This mad, ould fella at the side of the bed - starkers.

Wild eyes in a flushed face. Beard 'n' bristle.

Purple lips purring child-speak:

He-llooo! What did Santa bring you for Christmas?..

'Hasn't had a drink since. Hugh.

'Dry as the Sahara, 'that day to this.

'New man now. 'Goes to A.A., 'regular.

'Wife doesn't know herself.

 'Not that she sees that much of him!.. But still...

'Knows where he is, when to expect him,

that he'll be together when he shows...

That itself.... 'Has to be a bonus...

And the odd time we bump into each other,

his form is better than ever. No more bullshit.

And he says - giving me the eye -

If I can do it, anyone can do it...

———

Oh, he was a gonner. Well on the way - out.

And then, then... Santa Claus gave him sobriety.

Down the chimney, huh?.. Salvation in a stocking...

'At me to go along with him. An Open Meeting.

Don't have to say a word. Just sit tight, take it in...

Well... Maybe... Some dark night...

'Get there... slip in... 'circle of strangers...

Uptight among the Walking Wounded...

Listen to one, then another - men, women –

the old and the old-before-their-time -

tell how they came to on Skid Row,

struggled to their feet when the world

was ready to count them out...

Lemmings who turned - against all the odds -

to claw their way back up the sheer face

of a merciless cliff.

How did he manage it, Hugh? What was gifted to him?

What miracle was his, on-going?..

I'm going to lick this, I really am! I won't let it best me!..

Quietly, at his side, a fellow climber:

On your own? Hugh, you haven't a hope! Tell you what, though: we'll do it together…

Hmm… 'Worked for him. 'Works for some but not for others… And no one knows why or how, for sure…

Desperate. Determined… Clutching at straws – or gripping a lifeline?..

Well… some day… 'anonymous evening… Oh, that first time! Ugghhh… Fighting nausea. In knots, uptight, shaking…

M-Me?.. Oh-hh... I, eh... Well, I... I'm...
I did… I do… drink… drink too much…
No, I know, I know it's no solution.
Still, when everything's coming on top of me -
the roof caving in - it's easy enough to panic -
reach for a, a crutch...

Sorry?.. A - alone?.. Well, yes... I, I'd have to say - admit...
Oh, when she was out or away or up in bed, asleep. My
missus... A, a nightcap, you might say.

I, I'd stay downstairs and, and pour myself a, a...
One for the road, like... Huh?.. Or, or two...
Or - yes, until supplies ran out... Once,
once I start, I don't seem to be able to...
Yes. Yes, power. Yes. Power-less...

Sorry?.. Well, I had places in the house or outside -
where I knew she wouldn't - couldn't - get at it...
Hmmm?.. Oh, the Hard Stuff. 'Naggin. 'Half bottle.
Mebbe a bottle of plonk. Or two…
Behind the... or under, under the... or up over the -

Look, what the Hell does it matter where?!..
I had it, always made sure I had it! That's the - !
And yes, yes! I drank it! Alone!.. Secretly...

And when it was gone I got more! 'Always
had something in, stashed away - always!..
'Made damn sure... 'Wouldn't rest easy
unless I knew it was there... 'Couldn't!

What?.. Well, at first I'd be in rare form.
The giggles... 'Back to the good old days.
'Doing a turn for the lads.... Hilarious...

But then... after a while... I, I'd get angry.
With, with someone that wasn't there...
Someone, maybe, from the past
who had hurt me, done me wrong -
real maybe - maybe not...

Hmmm?.. Oh, furious. Vicious.
A torrent of verbal abuse,
destroying him - reducing her -
to a, a trembling, speechless wreck...

Eh-hh... Yes, I... 'Every... every night…
I, I stumbled up to bed... crying, maybe...
shagged... and always, comotose...

Devious. Deceit. Guile... I should have medals!..
'Never let my right hand know what my left is doing...
Cunning? A fox wouldn't be in it!
Denial? It's my middle name...
You could put it to me - straight up -
and I'd look you in the eye:
Are you joking? Me? Me!..
Minimise? If there was a degree
in minimising I'd fly it. No bother.
Honours! Oh, a Doctorate!..
And though she was way ahead of me -
Emma, I mean - well, most of the time -
when it came to covering our tracks,
I was cuter than her. Cuter than cute.

'Never thought I, I'd come out with it...
Confess. 'Not to a priest, in the darkness
of a confessional. But under lights, openly,
to a, a gathering of fellow - my fellow -
al-alcoholics...

Sorry?.. Yes... Yes, I... I can see that... now.

I... Yes, I am... am a... 'Have... have a...

Yes... Clear to me - now... Indeed...

There were two of us in it... And yes...

'Takes two... to Tango...

So many... I've lost so many yesterdays,

I, I don't want to lose Tomorrow...

No. none... There is no ser-serenity in my life...

Do, do something about it?.. Yes. 'Have to.

Jesus, yes. Stop. Now. Just - stop. No more.

Quit. Leave it... And I will, I will. Once I

make up my mind to -

What?.. Im-impossible?.. 'Don't stand a chance?..

On my own?.. Oh-hh... Oh, I... I...

We - we'll do it together?.. Oh-hhh...

Yes... Yes, I see where you're coming from...

Hello, yeah?.. Speaking... Yes?.. Oh, now I have you!
You were sitting next to Emma in that, that room - would I
be right?..

What?.. How do you mean, not with you any more?.. She
walked - out?.. Jesus... But I mean - where?.. It's a winter's
night, she hasn't a rex – that I know of...

Yes. Yes, I'm still here. Trying to take it in, that's all...
Now look, Miss eh - she was in your care, your
responsibility...

'Nothing you could do?.. Well, there bloodywell was!
You could have taken her clothes, shoved her under a cold
shower, locked her in a, a - something, anything!..

'Not like that?.. 'Not the way you do things?.. Is it not, be
God?..

If, if I hear anything I'm to let you know?.. Oh, good. Great.
If, if there's anything you can do?.. Terrific.
She didn't leave a forwarding address by any chance –
in case you want to send her a Progress Report?..

You, you're sorry for me?. Jesus, now I've heard
everything!.. Sorry for me?!

Look, Miss eh, whatever your name is:
if you and the rest of you in there hadn't been
so fucking merciless - so hard on me, on her –
if you hadn't come out with that bullshit
about roping in our wee one - my wife
might still be hanging in there!

'That ever occur to you - you stupid, sadistic bitch?!
Yeah, right... What?!.. Yes, I have medical insurance!
'Talk to you...

Shit!.. Oh, shit!..
So now... So there.
I have an absentee wife,
a distressed child,

44

a job in jeopardy,

an empty house -

and a drink problem...

Great. Terrific... Cheers.

Mmmm... You can have the key - and still be locked in...

Out there, somewhere... Oh, she'll manage...

'Always does... somehow... Forage, survive...

'Make a phone call... Cadge a lift...

bum a few quid... Scramble a taxi...

Crash down... 'One pad or another.

And in a day or two - or maybe three -

she'll move closer to base, survey the terrain,

circle a while… then land...

Sorry. I really am... And this time I mean it.

'Going to change... 'make a go of it... You'll see...

If, if you'll have me back... this once - more...

Yeah, sure... And the Moon is made of cheese.

Back, huh... Here. Home... Back to Square One.
Well, no... No, not quite...

 - *On your own?.. You haven't a hope...*
Tell you what, though: we'll do it together.

- *My, my name is John... I, I'm an alcoholic....*

- *God, grant me the courage... to change the things I can...*

- 'Gonna be a long haul.

- Hang in there, man.

- Mind how you go...

FAR SIDE OF THE MOON

Hello, is that Harry?.. Harry, this is Emma. Emma Byrne –
I was wondering if himself was... Sorry?..
I, I can't hear you very... Oh-hh... Oh no, that's all right.
He was probably ringing when I was... What's that?..
Yes, yes I'm sure he will.
All right, Harry... Good night...

Oh, what's the use!.. Even if he's there the lads behind the bar know the drill:

Haven't seen him all evening. Can I take a message in case he drops in?..

'That you, George? This is me, Emma... My husband's not
in the lounge by any chance?.. No. No chance...

Hello, Phil? Sorry for ringing so late but I - that's right,
Emma, Emma Byrne... He's not?.. Oh, well, thanks anyway
for checking... 'Nite...

'Must be in some other watering HOLE!..

Hello, Gus? Emma here... unit one two five, Valium Valley...
Y'know - the wife of your best customer...
I, I've just missed him?.. Oh, dear. Dear, dear, dear...
'Getting to be a habit, that... Just missing him by a -

They know the score, sure they do. Every barman for miles…
So here's to the Happy Wanderer! Here's to fifteen years of...

Here I am and there he is... still on the town...
with the boys... or the bird… doing his thing... his nut…
anything for kicks...

—

Do you blame me? For having a drink?
Ah, what the Hell does it matter!.. I'm alone,
that's what matters! Have been for a while now…
quite a considerable while...
And he doesn't give a damn... Cheers...

Oh, you don't have to be marooned on a desert island
to feel cut off...
You don't have to be in orbit to be out of it...
And no communication, none.

Oh, Emma! Emma, you stupid bitch!
Why can't you stop tormenting yourself? Why?!..

Love?.. I did, yes I did... once...
Living with him... every day... sharing…
anything from a nightcap to, to the same loo...
Just that...

But it goes down, deep inside you, like roots.
And it hurts, hurts like cruelest Hell, when...
when your other half begins to... to disengage...

He, he got to know my faults as I came to know his.
I did try... But you can't stop the clock...

Some day, some day he'll begin to go out of himself, too...

What was that!?..
Something?..
Oh, God... Oh, dear God...

Who's that?..
Is somebody there?..
Who is it?..

I... I hear things... nearly every night I...
Oh, I hate being on my own...
And I hate you! God, I hate you...

for what you're doing... to me...

So what do you suggest?..
Leave, quit, go my own way, start a new life -
mebbe head back to Rootsville?..
Is that what you're saying?..
'Not as easy as all that, Georgie boy...

So. So all right, then. Stay - but re-programme:
move out and about, mix, socialise, make new friends,
get involved, get out of yourself... 'That it?

Out of myself and into tennis,
Tupperware, bridge,
coffee mornings,
high teas on low stools,
sales of work and meals-on-wheels,
societies and circles and committees?

'That the scenario? 'That what you're putting to me?..
Ha... I'll keep to myself, thanks all the same,
grin and bear it.

You leave an empty house,
you get back to an empty house.
'Different if you have someone waiting...
if your partner's at base when you touch down...

But you're right, I really should go and talk things over...
someone who would understand, be able to, to...

Th-thank you for seeing me at such short notice...

Do you - is it all right if I, I smoke?.. Oh.

Oh, I see... No, no that's all right...

Well, yes I am, a little. Nerves, I suppose...

Y'see, I've never attended a, a... been to -

Sorry?.. Just, just relax and say the first thing that comes into
my head?.. Ha, ha!.. No, excuse me, I didn't mean to laugh.
It's just that if I do that - say the first thing that - well we, we
could be here all night! Ha, Ha - sorry...

I'm like that, y'see. Lately. I talk a lot, especially -
you'll smile when I tell you –
'specially to Harry and George and Phil...
Well, how the Hell do I know who they are?!..
They're just voices, that's all... 'reach me in my spaceship in
suburbia...

Hmmm?.. Yes, yes I am. Well, in a way... I mean, things
have... He, he's not who he was. And I - well, yes, I suppose -
I, I'm not the same as before... not quite the same as when we
started out...

Oh, just the one. A girl. Jennifer. But we all call her Jenny. Ah, she's a dote. Nine going on ninety - if you know what I mean... Oh, you'd be amazed at the things she comes out with. Old head on young shoulders. Pre-precocious, almost...

Yes, yes you could say that: 'loves to dress up... slip into my high heels when she gets the chance... To, to please? Oh yeah!.. Spot on... 'Bend over backwards, 'loves to please...

One way with me, one way with the teacher, one way with the woman next door, one way with her father - when he's around...

'Strong? No, no I wouldn't think so, not at all. 'Catches anything that's going. One cold after another... Frail wee one, really. But when she's well she's -

Blue eyes - sleepy, smiling, sad...
Curls and freckles framing a ha'penny nose.
Pleats bobbing in the wind...
Thin legs running, skipping, hop-hop-scotching
past our front window...

Why are you asking me about Jenny?..

This isn't about her - it's about me. And him.

Me and him. Us. The way we were, how it was, is...

what might have been...

Is, isn't that what this is all about?..

You, you want him to come here... with me... the two of us,

together... and then, then him to come back alone?.. Ha, ha!..

'You think he'd do that? 'You think for one moment he'd

drag himself away from his career, his pals, his booze to -

to?.. Ha, ha...

God, it took them all their time - the people in that place,

place where I was for a while - to get him to... 'Only when

they put a gun to his head - 'said it was for Jenny, for

Jenny's sake - did he...

Ah look, let's be honest: you don't know, I don't know... Your

guess is as good as mine...

So - do I pay your receptionist on the way out?..

'First time I ever paid cash for just saying whatever came

into my ha,ha! Well, I better go before... ha, ha! 'fore you

have a nervous breakdown!..

54

I never did keep that appointment, did I, Phil?..

No, no I didn't... And the librium?..

On prescription from a local doctor...

He mentioned something about hypertension.

I was to go back but I... The signal wasn't very strong...

got weaker and weaker...

'Phone?.. This hour?.. Who could be?.. Coming, I'm com - !

If it wakes Jenny I'll -

*Yes? Hello, yes?.. Cecil?.. No, there isn't... Yes, I think you
have... That's all right...*

He didn't say... Whoever he is, he's looking for Cecil.
Whoever Cecil is... 'Couldn't get off the line quick enough...
For a, a moment there I thought it might have been...
Oh, you fool, Emma! Emma, you fool!

Oh, I'll tell you, Phil: I saw the two days. 'Deed, yes!
'Went everywhere together. 'Wouldn't go without me.
Nor I without him. We were... inseparable...
Yes, Harry, yes!.. The memories are there…
full and plenty... intact... Great, wonderful times together!
The days and the nights, the seasons and the years...

There was a bond, there a marriage -
when I was his woman, he my man…
and I knew the fullness of him,
his joy in weakness after strenght,
sleep after passion...
before ever the clouds gathered
and the lightening struck...

I remember - ! Oh, no! No, I don't!..
I couldn't bear that...
I'll spare you, Gus - this barfly knows
when to switch off... spare myself...
the soul-searing torture of... riveting Recall…

—

56

You'll do for me yet. You will, y'know...

You're at it right this minute...

Leaving me, worrying me, fretting me... Cold war.

You don't respond anymore. No matter how hard I try,

you just won't let down the barrier...

It's beginning to tell. So congrats, mate,

you're doing a great job.

And there's not a law or a rule in the book

that can trip you up...

I, I curse you. Yes I do. I curse you from my heart!

I wish you the same aloneness you have inflicted on me!

I wish you every bleeding, agonising moment of it!

'You hear me, husband mine? I curse you!

Ah-hh!.. Oh-hh-hhh... Oh... No... No...

Just - just leave me...

That has to be good for a laugh - coming from me...
Oh, I've heard, read about it...
But I never thought it would happen to me...
never imagined you would raise your hand.

No. No, you don't hit a woman, no matter what...
So will you please... leave me... alone...

I - I could ring her. Lisa.

Lisa, can you meet me?..
I need to talk... Somewhere quiet... low lights.
I don't want anyone to see my face...
Yes, I know the place... About an hour?..
All right, then...

And she would, 'course she would
 And she'd understand, quite,
that I can't bear him to come near me,
touch me...

'Can't stand his presence, his breath...
'don't want to be in the same room,
breathe the same air…

———

Lisa. I hardly noticed her at first:

a quiet figure two, three bar stools away...

She turned to call for a fresh drink and our eyes met:

Lovely day. Indeed. If this keeps up for another while

we won't know ourselves...

This and that... Tentative taxi down the runway...

And then, of a sudden, take-off!

Vertical, it was so heady…

Oh, we hit it off - didn't we just!

She made me smile, laugh aloud.

Flitting from topic to topic in gay abandon...

Two glasses of white wine later

we were still in high gear.

And when she made to disengage –

Goodness, look at the time, 'must fly –

she pressed my hand in passing.

Electric, that first touch... Vibrant...

And as Frankie zoned in – bar-wiping - to sneer

a crudity about her in my ear I could have hit him!

Shit-shoveller! '*Wouldn't know a real lady from a dummy*

in C and A's!..

The following day, and the next, she didn't show.

A tinkering gin and tonic, then back here...

Then, towards the end of the week, when I walked in

she was - waiting, it seemed to me.

'Like a meeting of old friends after a long absence...

I kept, at first, an even keel, took stock:

two, three years younger;

fairer; voice lighter;

hair richer; slimmer -

though that, God knows, wouldn't be hard.

Again, take-off: rich, exhilarating conversation...

No sense of time, place... The only urgency to hold

on to her, keep her to myself as long as I could…

Her very nearness, physically compelling...

Tomorrow she was going to drive to the coast -
a quiet inlet that was a favourite haunt -
and would I care to join her?..

Oh-hh?... That sounds very... Well no,
I'm not doing anything tomorrow... Yes, I, eh...
I mean, it's very kind of you to... to...

(Emma? Emma are you sure you know what you're at?..
Oh, shut up! She's the best thing that's happened to me for
years - that's all I know, all I need to know. For now,
anyway...

But, but I mean - suppose?.. Anyway, she won't, I know she
won't... She knows I'm not into that, not at all... God, if she
made a pass at me?!..

Another drink and you'll want to go to the loo. Well? So?..
Well, suppose - when you excuse yourself, reach for your
handbag – she says, hold on a sec, I'll be with you..?
Oh... my... God...)

Lisa... Lisa, there's something I want to... You know
I'm married... well, like, supposed to be... and I, I...
How can I put it?.. I don't mean to hurt your feelings
- far from it... But, eh... Well, like, I - I just don't...
I mean I'm not... Eh-hh... Lisa, what I'm trying to say is,
I, I don't... Oh, God...

She pealed with laughter!..
'Know what, then? She leaned over, hugged me,
tilted and glanced against my cheek with her lips...

Hey, Frankie!.. Phil!.. George… Piss off. And you!
You at the end of the bar! Snug, smug, taking it all in -
feck off, foxy…
And you! You behind the venetian blinds across the way!
Just, just piss off!

And you!.. you especially...
you above all, husband mine...
Get lost, knotted...
You didn't give me a prayer,
not a hope of surviving on my own...

What a shock when the penny drops!
What a supercharged kick in the arse
you have coming to you!..

Emma's got a steady, you'll never guess...
Surprise, surprise!

Maybe a crony will ring you...
'Foxy drop it in your ear?..
A sealed note landing on your desk?..
Or you - you walk into your local
on the tail-end of a belly laugh?

Oh, I loved you... Really I did... Now... now I...

*Here, hold on - just a minute!... Lisa!.. Wait, will you?!
I can't keep up!.. L- i- s - a!?.. You said a walk - not a
feckin' forced march!..*

*- Come on, Emma! Shoulders back, swing your arms!..
Yes, okay, you're doing fine! Ah, that's my girl!..*

Wind on my face, in my hair,
as we walked,
marched,
scrambled,
stormed – oh, for miles and miles
of cliff-head and shore-line...

Back down to the pier:
rope and bollard, tack and tackle,
lobster pots and decaying seaweed...
A benevolent bench under a mounted life-belt.
Lisa. She stood above me, deep-breathing, intent,
framed by the slow rise and fall of still masts,
the canvassed criss-cross of boats at anchor...

And I knew, without her speaking a word,
what was in her mind, heart, for me...

'Get me out of myself... into shape... share with her –
books, poetry, music, theatre, travel.
Oh, a whole world I knew existed
beyond these four walls
but had thought, in my separation, not for me.

And we did... and we do...

Oh, wondrous hours of togetherness...

And not once, not once I swear,

over the past several weeks,

did she... as much as...

No, nothing. Nothing like that. . .

Friends. Oh, the best of... Rich enough for me,

contentment, indeed. But for her?.. I wondered...

Like to come back to my place?

Mmmmm. 'Love to...

A half-hour's drive away... Red-bricked, Victorian.

A better part of Flatsville… 'Dying to see her pad,

curious about her -

Ah, I might have known!

Creams and browns...

scatter rugs on parquet flooring...

wooden beams and old world motifs...

flowers and plants...

pastels and water colours...

fruit and garlic…

wine rack and salad bowl...

concealed lights framing stereo unit...

Oh, Lisa! Lisa, it's just you! -

I turned - exultant, congratulatory -

to find her reaching for me, embracing,

holding, encircling -

Oh, no... No, Lisa, no... Please, please don't...

Not, not on my lips... Not... on my...

No, don't... Please... Lisa... Lisa?..

Oh, Lisa. Lisa, it's un-un-UN-NA... Ah-hhhhh... hhh...

Is it?.. Who says so?..

Tell them from me they're wrong - way out.

Two in love, loving. Ah yes, that. Of course, yes.

Two not in love - then travesty... blasphemy.

Long, long winter. Spring soon... Reprise.

Flower coming out of soil… moist.

'Never the same... ever.

'Quite the same... never.

So she knew. Sensed it all along.

Probably from our very first meeting.

That there was this in me,

that I was more - or less - than I made out to be...

that I was what I had sought to suppress,

refused to admit,

even in my most secret moments...

that I was… deep down...

Bitch! Oh Lisa, you bitch!

Exciting, scintillating, irresistible,

adorable, pure whore of a canny bitch!

You knew. From the very - !

Maybe that's why he takes off, night after night...
stays away... sleeps with his back to me, snoring...
or in the other room, snoring?..
The vibes are wrong?.. Ah, to Hell with him!..

Of course I'm shaking... Trembling all over...
So... where do we go from here, my lovely?..
Explore?.. Experiment?.. Press on?.. Press?..
Is this what you want, Lisa?..
Me to be a man to your woman…
woman to your man?..

Some would deem the very suggestion
coarse, crass, obnoxious. .. Some? Oh, many -
the many who would shudder, shun, ostracize...
gladly see us out of this world...
commit us to perpetual exile...

But inadequate? Never!

The inadequacy was here. Here!

Upstairs, downstairs, in your lady's chamber!

A dash to the line: Sprint! Spurt!..

Oh, he would never make a long-distance runner,

my husband: no harrier, he!

Never worked at it, never!

'Sought to make it the sublime experience

that it would be, could be, if only he had...

Only when he was in the mood... when it suited him…

when he felt the urge…

Upstairs, downstairs, in me your lady's chamber!..

Leaving me brutalised... sleepless…

lip-biting… wet-eyed in the dark...

wondering was it me, my fault?..

Your doing, this! Your doing!

You left the door wide open!

Or mine?.. Maybe… Maybe my..?

Oh, what does it matter, any more?..

Lisa's in my life now... is my life!..

Emma?.. Emma, look at me... Come on, look up...

Here, I'm here... Lisa... Yours... Your Lisa...

Here, beside you... Always will be... if you'll have me...

Oh, no. Please don't...

I can't bear to see the fear in your face,

apprehension in your eyes!..

Journey into the unknown: suppose, suppose
it does not work out? 'That it?
'That what you're thinking?..
Oh, Emma, Emma! Don't be afraid!..

If we go forward, hand in hand,

bound in wholehearted committal,

we will succeed, you'll see!..

You could get a job, too - even part-time.

I've got some savings, we'd manage...

'Able to use your own name again.

And you'd be safe, sheltered, secure...

I would never leave you, never!

You have my most solemn word on that...

Yes. Yes, I've had affairs in the past,
I won't deny it - two, three.
But never lasting... never the same promise,
assurance... that this, this...

I won't force you, sister, won't pressurize...
'Take it as it comes - a step, stage, day at a time...
To fall asleep at night... under the same roof...
in each other's arms - oh, glorious solace -
would be beginning enough...
You don't need the services of a man - any more than I do!..

You want the comfort of a friend,
the backing of a partner...
support, assurance... mutual allegiance.
I can see the great good in you -
what you could be, given half a chance...
'Not your looks - though in my eyes,
you are truly lovely.
No, don't laugh! You really are...
It's you, the person you are, that I love...

Emma, my Emma.

Oh, we'll fight, you may be sure of it -
blazing rows, full throttle... These eyes -
eyes you zone in on so much - can flash fire!

But we would weather the storm, Emma...
the clouds would blow over, soon enough...
and we would never, ever, inflict fear -
much less physical force - on each other...

What more can I..? Emma?..
You - don't you see what I...
Emma?.
'What I, I'm trying to?..
Emma?..

I kissed her, then… on the mouth, full…

her lips, my lips… and knew as she responded -

sighing, touching, clinging -

that I would never, ever, be the same again...

Lisa... Lisa!.. L-I-S-A-A-A-A!..

Well… if a full moon can draw an ocean,

reduce it to seawash on shingle,

then who am I to say yea or nay

to the surge within me?..

Is there a Lisa?.. Does Jenny exist?..

And you?.. Are you out there somewhere?..

How real is real?..

Meaning I am - loony?.. But I'm not, am I?.. Luna.

Look, Luna, I'll tell you: I, I'm every bit as sane

as the next bi-bi-bi-sexual.

Chance. Chance encounter. Chance awakening of...

Lisa's choice... piece of cake… lucky me...

Heaven. Admission free... Free!?..

Ah, feck you, Lisa! Feck you, anyway!

I was wishing, praying to God, hoping against hope

that - that the moon was made of cheese…

Back off, you cow! How dare you!..

Ask - demand to know - where I've been -
how long I stayed - whom I met!..
Don't!.. Don't hedge me, curtail my -
I won't abide it, do you hear?..

I cannot take your
overriding
overruling
overbearing
overwhelming
total and complete possessiveness
of me – Lisa!
of me – Emma!
of me - Lisa!
Emma!.. Lisa!..

I... Look, I… I'm sorry... I didn't mean to...

Here, come on... dry your... 'Not like me to...
God, they'll think we're a right pair,
the people next door...

Just - try to see it from my…

I've been alone - on my own - so much...

'Course I love being with you...

But sometimes I, I like to go my own way,

do my own thing...

Do you - can't you understand that?..

No. No, there's no one else. Trust...

Trust each other? Remember?..

Oh, why does there always have to be a reason,

explanation..? Why... always... a price..?

Here... where I am now… with him, without him...

the odds are enormous... the price, confinement...

Badgered... bullied, cowered.

Or clawing back, daring, defiant.

'Best form of defence, sometimes.

What do you mean, I've had enough?
Are you off again?
God, will you look who's talking?!..
I will if I bloodywell like!..

And for all his ranting and raving,
I nearly always get the better of him.
'Bide my time, wait till he's off-guard -
then go for the jugular...

Ssssshhh... Men, huh! I enjoy provoking the bastards!..
So much I relish the triumph of verbal castration!

No. Oh, no. No question...
I mean, were I really an alcoholic
I would be capable of - of
lying,
cheating,
fabricating,
deflecting,
changing...

Changing?..

———

They say it does things to your mind. Body…
A few drinks and - snap!.. Cut, slash...
Easy to take on, annihilate,
someone who isn't really there...

No illusions about Lisa. .. And no doubt
about how it will be in, in outer space…
Out to improve me. Take-over...
Where he failed, she - determined lady - will succeed.

For all that, I'd be lost without her...
'Love every fibre, freckle, curve, inundation
of the body that has brought my body to
throbbing, vibrant life - as never before...

Oh, the pleasure!
The prospect of the pleasure!..
The sheer,
unmitigated joy
of ongoing,
undying,
uninterrupted
coupling...

Bless me, Father, for I have sinned...

It's light years since my last confession, Father -
and about ten seconds since my last grevious sin...
in thought, word... through my fault, through my fault.

My, my husband doesn't find me attractive any more -
through my fault.
I've driven him away from me, from our home...
driven him to drink, to other women...
through my most grievous fault.

I, I drink too much and I've put on weight
and my hair is thinning and he finds my conversation dull
and I put a brake on his freedom, he says,
and he finds me an embarrassment in company -
mea culpa, mea maxima...

Father, I, I've decided to stop the lights...
cut out the sham... quit putting on an act.

78

'Start, instead, to just - just be myself...

'way God made me...

'Thought I'd let you know… see what you think...

Maybe get... maybe even get...

some sort of a, a blessing?

Young. Young cleric. 'Knew by his voice: *I know...*What do you know? Father. Really?..

God loves… forgives us... no matter what.

He sees us, warts and all... sees into us.

On the Cross, arms outstretched,

he continues to forgive...

On-going, all-encompassing embrace...

He loves, forgives, each and every one of us

with a limitless compassion...

You have only to turn to him

to find him already turned to you…

I know that, Father. 'Believe it, most of it, I think…

Oh, Emma, you had better!

'Your only life-line when the sands run out...

'Trouble is, Padre, I find it well-nigh
impossible to forgive - me...
grant myself the cleansing illusion
of absolution.

You only get on the roundabout once!..
Ah, but Lisa, what a way to go!..
Go... quit... split... Leave...
Walk - on, out, away. Just - go!..
'You think it's as easy as that?..

Will I, won't I?..

One way, then the other...
one way, then the other...
one way, then the other!
Then the other way,
now this way!..
No, not there - here...
Not over here - there!
There now!.. Here and now!
Yes and no!

Hi!.. With it... all hang out... laid back... hyped... leg it...
crash out... cool...

The in-words that didn't even exist when I was -
hop-hop-scotching down our street,
pigtails bobbing in the wind,
freckles framing a ha'penny nose...

How was I to know, then,
that it was only a matter of chromosomes -
a gene or two, give or take?..

But that was a long time ago, if ever...
A world - oh, a galaxy! - away...
And now it is night,
the hour of the lone star,
of the solitary constellation...

Here's to the Centre!
Centre for the treatment of, of
the Walking Wounded...
Here's to the several Counselors who thrive there -
Centre of their Universe...

May they slumber in serenity

through the hours of night...

till the dawn chorus summons them

to rise and shine… smile at another day…

go to it... form a Circle...

reduce some other, unfortunate alco

to, to sheerest shit.

But not me. Oh, no. No, no, no! Never again...

No! Let go of me! Let-go-of-me!..

I won't, I won't!.. Don't want to, want to -

Jenny? Jenny, don't let them!

Get away from me! Get-away-from-me!..

Don't let them take me away, love!..

Oh, no! Jesus, will no one help me?..

You bastard! May you burn in Hell for -

Oh, God… Oh, dear God...

Is that the way of it, then?

Has it come to this?..

Jesus, you sign that paper

and I'll hate you to the day I die...

'My last breath I'll curse you...

———

Jenny?.. Jenny, I'm home!.. Y-e-sss!..
Your Mummy's home to you, love!..
Ah, come here to me... Can I have a hug?
'Course I can...

Oh, Jenny, Jenny, Jenny! My girl, aren't you?
Sure, you are!
And I'm your Mummy that won't ever leave you.
Never, ever, again.

Did you miss me, sweetie? 'Course you did...
But sure I wasn't away all that long, now was I?..
Oh, they wanted me to stay on but I said no,
my wee one's at home with no Mummy
to look after her. So...

Here, have you still got a few tickles left, eh?. .
Oh, now, I think you might have, Jenny, hmmm?..

"Round and round the garden... like a Teddy Bear... one step... two steps... tickle me under there!.."

Goodness, look at the state of this...

Oh, dear. Mummy's got lots to do...
Now, two biscuits out of the tin
and out you go to play -
sure, it's a lovely Summer's day...

Oh-hh-hhh. .. Stagnation.
Me and the four walls.
The radio. . . television.
Slow decline.
Monotonous descent into
uselessness.
End fruitless existence
staring dull-eyed, glazed,
at the frightening - frightened -
baggage
in a geriatric ward...
No!.. Oh, no!.. No, no, no!..

Lisa?.. Oh, thank God!.. Lisa, listen. I - I've got to get
away... Soon be… Him. Soon be here... Oh, would you?
Would you, my darling!?.. About an hour - get a few things
together... Just as I am?.. Oh-hh... All right. All right, then…
I - I'll look out for your headlights…

And she will, I know she will...
Just waiting for my call,
hoping I get the courage to, to...

All right, so I'm angry - guilty...
Look, I've had it, understand?
Had it! Up to here!..
I'm sick of don't do this and don't do that
and do, do the other!..

And I'm sick - oh, so sick - of being
watched,
guarded,
noted,
indexed,
filed,
an-al-ysed!

Not a bad semi, this...
Almost a showhouse when we got it...
Ah, but we let it go down. He did... No, I did.
Keep it nice? For who?.. No interest, none.

He had it right, for once:
when I stood at the kitchen window,
staring at the overgrowth
that could have been a garden,
I was focused on a far further distance -
beyond the partition wall,
the rooftops of the next row,
up and away to a shadowy world
that drew me, irresistibly...

So... goodbye, Frankie… George... Phil...
Goodbye, Foxy - ferret-eyes...
Good luck, little people...
the savoury gravy brigade...
To-ing and fro-ing. . .
in and out of your warrens in
Valium Valley, Librium Groves, Enema Heights...

And goodbye you -

you useless piece of beer-bellied flotsam!

I cosseted you far too long...

Now look to your own socks, shirts, underwear -

see to your own smell!

'Know how to cook potatoes? You boil them...

How to empty a vacuum cleaner?

Clear a drain? Change a plug... wheel?..

Grill a chop, fry an egg?..

Re-place a bulb, paint a wall, ring for services –

Where am I?..

Oh, you poor bastard...

so much you brought upon yourself...

because of me - ME...

The way I am... 'way I have been, maybe, all my life -

though I didn't know it until...

'Way you wouldn't understand,

not in a million years...

Better this way - oh, by far!..
'Would have destroyed you... 'destroyed each other...
And Jenny... Ah, yes. 'Above all, Jenny...
She especially... particularly.

She, she'll be all right. I know she'll be all right...
Rita, Rita will be good to her. And Missus Kane in 129...
And his sister - 'bout time she showed an, an interest.
I know, I know it will work out...
And it's not as if... I mean, it'll only be for...
She'll understand... when she gets, gets a bit older...
'See it differently... 'Know that, that it was the only way...

'Course I'll come back for her... 'soon as I, I settle. . .
get a bit, get things right...
And we, we'll be happy, happy together...
Sure she loves Lisa. And Lisa, Lisa I know loves her...
'Give her a whole new - 'Give her the world!

And she'll forget, sure she will, forget in time -
about here… and him… and this, this
semi-detached patch of,
of inconsequential do's and don'ts...

Oh-hh! You're not thinking of going without..?

No. No, of course not...

'Ease into her room, one last...

Night light, warm glow… Linger a while…

Jenny and her dolls, dreams...

Feather kiss on baby cheek...

Yes! Oh, yes!..

A last, lingering look that will stay with me all my -

No! No such thing - you mustn't!

One glance at those eye lashes and you won't be able -

ever be able to, to -

But I want to, Lisa!.. My baby!.. want to...

Emma! Emma, are you listening to me?!..

'Love you, Jenny! Love you to bits!

The sun, the moon and the stars.

So much I love you - and always will.

She'll leave you, Emma, yes she will!..
You mark my words: a few short years from now
she'll go, split, emigrate... And you, you'll be left -
and it will be too late, too late to, to...

Yes. Yes, I see what you... Of course, yes...
You, you'll be all right, love... Mummy has to go away for a
while but she'll be back, never fear, no matter what...

H - E - YYY!.. Diddle, diddle...
The cat... and the... fiddle...
The little dog laughed... to see such fun...
And the dish... ran away...
with the... spoon...

- Re-programme... re-programme!..
Safety belt - clink, clank...
Fire all rockets!
- All rockets?
All... We won't be coming back...

Jettison all baggage.

- All useless baggage?

All baggage...

Five… four... three… two...
We have ignition!

Steady, old girl!

- Steady as you go, Lisa!

Ragdoll overboard, Emma!

- What? But, I - I...

Do it. Now!..

No, don't look back! Don't ever look back...

It doesn't just happen, you make it happen!..

You make your way by taking it!..

We're heading for outer space, sister!

- Just you and me and the stars!

Beyond the Milky Way!

- Far side of the Moon!..

DEAD MAN TALKING

Hello?.. Patricia?.. Ah-hh... Bearing up, just about...

No word, no?.. No... I was hoping you might have... No...
'Waited up half the night... Unless she showed during the
day? Well, she has her own key... 'knows bloody well I'm at
work...

Four days now. And nights... Not fair, not a bit fair
on the wee one... Ah, you wouldn't know, Patricia.
Wasn't a word out of her getting ready for school –
another morning you couldn't shut her up...
Oh, she'll be all right till I get home, it's just for now...

Look, I'll scramble, Pat... Just clearing my desk.
With a bit of luck I'll beat the traffic...
Oh, and if you hear anything - even a whisper –
you'll let me - Ah, you're a brick...
You, too... 'Bye, Pat. 'Bye.

 Oh, Emma, Emma... Bitch. Bitch to do this on me... on our Jenny...

Jenny?.. Jenny, I'm home!.. Jenny?.. You up there, kiddo?..
Jenny?!..

Hmmm... 'Must be gone out... Round in Wards, maybe, or
      across in McHughs... 'Can't say I blame her...

What a mess... what a bloody awful - Oh-hh?.. Left me a...

———

Dear Dad... I am over in Quinns.

I am doing my homework with Deirdre.

I will watch out for your car.

I have set the table.

I dont know whats for tea.

Please find Mummy and bring her home.

I love you Dad. Hugs and kisses.

Jenny.

Not bad... Not bad for a nine-year-old - going on ninty...

Well, I'll try, kiddo... 'Easier said than done...

Mummy, huh... Mummy...

I could try Clearys?.. Liam'll be there for sure,

always drops in for a scoop on his way home...

Or the Harbour Bar?.. Joe never misses – and *he* can hear the

grass growing. If anyone has wind of anything stirring it'll be

Joe -

Ease in the side door, catch his eye, give him the beck, buy him a pint, a word in his ear at a quiet table...

Good luck a while...

Cheers, Joe - whatever that means...

Jeez, it's rough all right, no doubt.

So... What's the story?

 Well... it seems this bird drifted into the area a few weeks ago. 'Not just stranger - strange.

How do y'mean?

Ah, y'know - not like another.

'Not the eh, marrying type?

Now you have it. I'm trying to keep my voice down.

Go on.

So it seems your missus met up with her. In a pub.

Where else?.. So?

So they took a great shine to each other. And that's how it's -

Any idea where they are now?

The word is, they're still around. But where I just don't -

———

This one - is she flush?

Money no object, from what I can gather. 'Spending as if it was going out of fashion.

Hmmm... 'Have to make tracks. Thanks for the info -

No problem. I'll let you know if I hear -

You have my number.

To be honest with you, if she was my missus I'd be up for assault.

Why do you think I'm looking for her?..

Was he..? Was Joe trying to tell me something?.. Ah, not at all... Emma?.. Emma?!.. My wife?.. Don't be mad!.. I know her, know her form... We, we share the same bed, damnit..

'Nothing to it... Booze, that's all. Free booze and a good time... That's all that's... Unless?.. Ah, no... Ah, Jesus, no!.. Well, shag you, Joe... Shag you, anyway...   for planting it in my...

- *Oh*, Daddy -

- There, there a leana -

- Daddy, Daddy -

- Schhh, now, schhh...

- If, if Mummy can't get in -

- Nice and warm, aren't you? -

- When we, we're asleep -

- Well, I won't lock the back door, Jenny, simple as that -

- Promise. Promise, Daddy -

- Your Mummy? That loves you? And you love her. Never! No way would I do such a thing!

- Oh, Daddy! Daddy, I love you!

- And I love you, sweetheart. Come on now. Big long sleep...

- Once, Daddy, once when I got home from school I, I was locked out -

- Oh, no! Dear, dear, dear...

- And I didn't know what, what to do -

- Well, it won't ever happen again, Jenny -

- On your word of honour?

- Honest to God -

- All right, then -

- Not you, not your Mummy - no one will ever be locked out of this house, ever again!

- Good boy, Daddy -

- Okay?

- Okay, Daddy -

- Wee wet blue eyes... 'Got enough tissues?

—

- Ah, ha -

- Come on, then. Tuck in, nice and warm -

- You, you won't go out - ?

- No, I'll just be downstairs -

- 'Won't close my -

- No, I won't close your door, Jenny -

- And will you come to bed? -

- Yes, I'll be going to bed, too. Very soon. Now, I'll just lower your light, just a little, okay?

- Okay... Oh, and Daddy, Daddy!?

- Hmmmm?

- You will call me - ?

- Don't I always? 'See you in the morning, sunshine...

- See you... in the... morning...

- Sleep tight, sweetheart.

- My Daddy, aren't you?

- That's for sure. And always will be -

- No matter what.

- No matter what...

'Frets in her sleep... Every night lately…

I listen on the landing: a wee cry... soft, sad whimper.

'Wait for her to turn, drift into Dreamland,

sucking her thumb, inevitably…

And what'll it be like in the morning if she doesn't show? Ah, feck you, Emma, feck you, anyhow. 'Tried anywhere I could think of - every dart board for miles… Even places I wouldn't be caught dead in. Not a trace...

God Almighty, what'll she try next?.. Taking up with a, a... One, mebbe, as mad as herself. 'Don't even know her name. Nor want to. If she has a car and credit cards she's elected. For now, anyway. Or till the well runs dry...

Huh. Maybe I should try ringing a four-star hotel:

Hello, Reception? I wonder could you tell me, do you have two wild women in the lounge by any chance?..

The last Jenny saw of her, she was only going as far as the dry-cleaners - that was four days ago!

Jesus, I could swing for her this minute... All the same, if there was something wrong?.. Ill, maybe..? An accident..? I wouldn't like to...

Ah, ould Ned had it right that night in O'Dwyers - hit the nail on the head...

Here, get that into you and we'll face the world together.

Cheers, Ned. Good luck a while.

So... Ye had a row, huh?

If you could call it that...

Oh-hh? No prisoners, eh?

She, she stormed out...

Ah, now... God made ye and God matched ye -

Do you reckon?

No two ways about it... Lookit here to me: your missus – and I know her well, many's the jar I stood her, many's the head-to-head we had - reminds me for all the world of, of...

Hmmm?..

*Do y'see, there was a neighbour o' mine, a farmer - oh,
years and years ago - had this cow. The best milker in the
herd, she was. Mornin' after mornin' - rain, hail or shine -
she'd give him a full pail...*

What are you on about - ?

*Ah, but she was wayward. An unmanageable, pure hoor of a
baesth, entirely. As soon as she was milked, she'd flail out
with her hind legs and kick the bucket to Hell ou'a that...*

Ah, I'm with you now!

*I'm tellin' ya, worse than useless! 'Broke his heart, the same
animal...*

To a T, had her to a T...

Emma, huh?.. Emma, the champion milker!..

Pure whore of a wayward cow!..

Her, all right... For sure...

Out there somewhere, roaming... Ah, if ever there was a
maverick!

Oh, yes, sure: good woman in ways - good turn in her - but give her the smell of a cork and...

Oh, I was hoping... that time she went in, checked herself in, into the Centre -
hoping, praying to God - it would be the makings of her, 'bring her to herself...

Ah, but she didn't stay the course, stick the pace. 'Picked a row with one of the Counselors, upped and left... walked out the main gates into a winter's night...

In a few days she was back... here.
We were all back - to Square One...

Hello, yeah?.. Ah, hello, Pat... Huh?.. What are you on about?..
Come on, no beating around the bush! Just tell me - straight up...

What!?.. Hmmmm...

Yeah, no, I'm still here... Just, just thinking...
'You sure the tickets were one-way - certain?..
So... so what do they do - fly on from London?..
Hmmm... When - what time was that?.. I see...

Oh-hh... pour meself a large one... wish them bon voyage...
mebbe finish the bottle...

No! No, I won't! 'Have to be on the ball in the morning.
Anyway, I'm glad it was you that... 'Better than getting it
thrown in my face by some...

Oh, I can tell, know by your voice...
One Helluva phone call...
But look, much appreciated, all right?..

Ah, not to worry, I'll manage. Work a few things out...
No, we'll leave it at that. Please. For now...
Please. I just want to... Yes...
Keep in touch, huh?.. You, too... Good night.
'Night, Patricia.

Joke... It's a joke, right?.. Sick, sick joke... But still a jo - ?
Yes?.. Yes?!. No?.. No.

So... where do we go from here, my lovely?..

Jesus... Jesus wept. 'Bet he didn't talk to himself - or did
he?.. Ah, now! You could be at a lot worse - better than
talking to some gobshite...

Well for him - able to weep... cry. 'Wish I could. It would be
a relief... 'Can't, can't remember the last time I shed a tear.
Or two... I'm past it. When - when it hurts so much you can't
cry, that's pain. Pain de la Pain...

Laugh? Ah, well, now, that's a different story. So... you say
to your man at the bar:

*Here, here's one for you: what vegetable goes with tears,
crying, eyes watering?..*

And he'll say –

Onion. Onions.

And you say -

Onions? Onions?!. No one ever give you a belt in the goolies with a turnip?..

Oh, you've blown it, Emma, this time you've really...

If... if you'd fecked off with a man - any man, no matter who - that atself, it wouldn't have been so bad... Maybe a young buck who could do more for you than I ever could... Or a fella with oodles and lashings, promising a non-stop, merry-go-round.

I could have taken that - I think. Oh, not without a lash across the face, but still. I might just have survived. Maybe.
But Jesus, Emma!.. To go off with a - !

Now come on!

The Twelve Tribes of Man laughing at me:

The gin-and-tonic cartel,

the bottle brigade and the pint men,

the wee Jemmies and the large Paddies –

all getting it up for me because,

'cause I wasn't able... to hold on... to my woman.

And I can't do a thing about it - 'can't split, take off,

disappear, run for cover... Not with a wee one... 'wee one

clinging to me, wandering into my bedroom of a morning,

blue eyes filled with tears, shaking... rousing... asking –

Where is my Mummy?..

And when I'm at work, trying - trying the best I can - to hold

down a job because there maybe won't be another...

And she is home from school,

uniformed but far from uniform,

staring, dull-eyed, at a text-book

that means far less to her than her mother's whereabouts,

she has nothing - do y'understand? - nothing in this front

room except dust and disorder... and colour... TV...

'Any wonder that she loses herself in it?
Any wonder that it means more to her
than the verb to be,
adding and subtracting,
sixteen nine nought
the Battle of the Boyne was fought -
the Lakes of Killarney,
the rivers of Europe,
the mountains of the Moon?..

And I try - at least I try –
not to transmit to her...
the way I feel... about you.

Jesus, Emma, how could you?..
Your wee one, 'own daughter,
flesh and blood, jettisoned.
You, you dumped her –
the way you would a, a rag doll.

Gone... Bag and baggage - and passport...
Why?.. Why! We could have worked something out,
compromised... give and take... salvaged, saved...
kept it together - somehow...

———

But we never talked, did we? Not really.

Not of late. Just - shouted.

'Went our different ways...

I'd say you were only pissed out of your mind

getting on that plane - would I be right?..

Sure we all have a fling, now and again,

here and there... going through life...

if, if you're anyway half lucky.

'Fair enough. Par for the course.

But God Almighty! To go off the rails altogether!

Put a final, irredeemable full stop

at the end of a broken sentence!

No matter how you look at it:

six thousand miles is a long way to go

to get - nowhere.

Hello, yes?.. Hello!.. HEL- LO?!.. Hmmmm...

Funny how the line goes dead when I answer. Hilarious...
One of her many admirers... Some poor, unfortunate ejiit
who thinks the sun, moon and stars shine out of her arse.
So the word hasn't reached him yet, the penny hasn't
dropped..?

Huh. He has it coming to him - a belt in the goolies with a
turnip. 'Not the first time she brought the tears to a man's
eyes...

I don't... I just don't... This couldn't be happening to -
Oh, you better believe it, lad! Cut. Split. Gone. Vamoose.
End of Act I...

All around, the bits and pieces, fractures and fragments,
desolate debris of a... direct hit. Wasteland...

And all because she - she wouldn't stop. Mebbe couldn't, I
dunno... Or didn't really want to... Which? If any?.. But don't
try to tell me the one had nothing to do with the other: I
won't wear it...

One of her doctors - she went through a few - told me once that when it comes to alcohol anything - but anything - is possible. I should have paid him for that... He forgot to add, even - even - Mad Cow Disease.

I, I didn't notice at first - I think... 'Lot of things I didn't notice, those days. God, wasn't I hard at it myself? 'Well got in my local, regular as clock-work. Sure if I didn't show they'd send up flares...

And she, she could hold her own in any company. A good-looker, vivacious, vital. When she flowed into a lounge bar they bet each other off, near enough, to buy her a drink, claim her company... At first... at first.

And if Jenny was in tow, on display, it was a coke and crisps and play outside, that's the good girl, Mummy will be with you in a minute... or an hour... or two.

A fag in one hand, a glass in the other, on a high stool, a good four feet - oh, light years! - removed from terra firma.

I heard - listened ad nauseum - to the contrived excuses,
futile promises, meaningless apologies:

You'll never believe... Look, I'm sorry... It's just that...
'Wasn't my fault... I mean, how was I to know?.. It won't
happen again... I promise... And this time I really mean it...

Really?.. Yeah, sure. And the Moon is made of cheese.

I heard - though I didn't want to hear - the repetitious
bullshit, the senseless, aimless, argumentation, the nasal
slurring, the deadly delusions of grandeur...

I heard - how could I not hear? - the strident, high-pitched,
demand for order and excellence - why isn't that done,
this finished, the other ready? - when, eventually, she made it
back to base.

And Jenny, in her room, trembling, in tears...

'Heard, on the grapevine, that she had been barred – here, then there.

'Heard the voice of a well-wisher in my ear, trotting out the hallowed cliché -

I think she has a problem...

You think? You bloodywell know! Which means, I have a problem!..

I saw - but I didn't want to see –
the cigarette burns,
the damage to the car,
the pills, capsules, prescriptions, medical - hospital - bills,
off-license chits, supermarket empties, parking tickets,
final demands, letters and cards and messages from people
I didn't even know existed...

And then, then there was the classic refrain:

If only, if only... we could move, start again somewhere else... things would be soooo different...

The house was wrong, the road, the neighbourhood, the
people next door, them across the way...
Everything would be just fine once we switched to a -
a flat in town,
a bungalow by the sea,
a castle in Spain,
a starship on Mars...

The counsellors at the Centre were duly gutted: sadists, the
lot of them, no understanding, none, no milk of human
kindness.

And over those cold days and nights, how many of her palsy
walsies went to see her?.. None. Ne'er a one.

Not that she stayed long - but long enough to collect a few
'phone numbers, contacts from fellow travelers... Oh no, she
didn't believe in wasting time: if you're in, kiddo, make the
most of it...

'**W**alked into this pub one day and asked for a pint - of drug. The look on your man's face behind the bar! Of all drugs, the most socially acceptable...

Would you go along with that, Emma?.. Call it what you will - give it a catchy name, an attractive label - when the chips are down, it's a drug.

Yes. Yes, indeed... 'Hooked... And with no real wish to get off the hook. 'Won't... or can't... Or maybe you just don't want to... discuss it... want to know.

Or - or could it be something else again, something deeper?.. I dunno - I'm no head shrinker - but I'm willing to bet you were drinking because you were drowning, trying to drown, the other, deeper, persona that was in you.

'Trying, desperately, to walk on the same side of the street as everyone else, the other women of your ken...

'Seeking to suppress the force that was growing and mounting in you all the while... 'Knowing, deep down, sooner or later, the floodtide would burst its banks, overwhelm you, me, all that lay in its path.

Emma? Would I be right?.. Emma?.. Or not too far off-target?.. Hmmm?.. Bullseye?.. What do you say, Emma?.. Yeah, I reckon... Bullseye...

Time, what's the..? Coming up to closing. If I move now I'd get in before last orders - they'd give me one, I know they'd give me one - mebbe two... Two creamies and, and a chaser. Yes. Yes!

'Need to talk to someone... Frank could be there? Or Charlie? Charlie for sure... Come on, then. Move it!

Eh-hh... Jenny?.. Too late to try for a baby sitter... She, she'll be all right. Fast asleep. Chances are she won't wake till morning... Yes. 'Back in jig time. Phone off the hook... Occasional lights on... Back door locked... Switch on stereo... low...

Right, then... Ease her down the driveway... Lights, ignition... Put down the boot...

But, but if she does..? Suppose, just suppose she wakes..? Fretting... Bad dream... 'Comes down... holding the bannister, rubbing her eye?..

Yeah... No. No, better not. The chances are she won't - but then again, she might... I'd never forgive myself if... Nailed, huh? Caught... Hmmmm... 'That you laughing at me, Emma? Sneering?.. Jeering? One up on me, huh?

Well, I'll tell you this for nothing: I'm going to climb out of this wreckage, walk away from this crash! Salvage everything I can... 'Come out of it, maybe, a better man, 'better than ever I - and to Hell with you, you bitch!

Ah, is it yourself! Be God, I haven't laid eyes on you

in a month o' Sundays!.. Hidin' on me, were you?..

Or just keepin' the head down?..

Well, I don't have to tell you,

you're lookin' the worse for the wear...

Not that anyone'd blame you.

'Deed I did. The jist of it, anyway...

Sure the dogs in the street have it by now!..

Ah, don't be talkin'! 'Shockin', no doubt. 'Bates all...

But sure there y'are, that's the way,

you never know what's round the corner...

Lookit here to me:

we all have our problems - haven't we, just!..

The one God sent me, do y'think she'd budge?

Not a hope! I have her mornin', noon and night –

under me feet, breathin' down me neck, till death do us part.

If she's not complainin' she's moaning,'

if she's not whingin' she's whinin',

if she's not grousin' she's grumpin'.

If ever there was a perpetual pain in the arse!

Is it any wonder I'm out

more than I'm in?

Be God, I'll be dug out of her yet!..

Do y'know what I'm goin' to tell ya?
It's down on your knees you should be,
thankin' the Almighty for a merciful deliverance
from such a, a Towering Inferno!..

Ah, no doubt! What is it - four, five weeks?
Even as it stands, you're over the worst of it!..
Sure you won't know yourself after another while!

But mark my words: easy come, easy go.
If this new set-up turns sour
she could be back on your doorstep
before you'd know where you were...
Take my advice, a mhic,
and get yourself a good solicitor.
Aye, and the sooner the better...

Thank . . . thank you for seeing me at such short notice.
Yes, a friend... close acquaintance... put me on to you - eh,
recommended. I understand you specialise in this sort of...

Well, I can't say I envy you... No, no shortage of clients?..
Well, I dare say - that does not surprise me. Anyway...

Yes, of course. To business. 'Fact is, it's final, just about as
final as it could get, I suppose. I, I've given it a lot of
thought - as you can imagine - so, so the first thing I want to
do is, is sell the house...

How, how do y'mean?.. What!.. 'Her con-consent...
signature?.. But she's not even in the country, damnit!..
How do I know where?!.. And anyway, what has she got to
do with it? My money, my house!

It was me - me paid the deposit,
got the mortgage,
made the repayments,
cleared the H.P. on the furniture,
went to the Credit Union,
raised the loan for the - me!

All she ever put into it went down the loo –
or out in the bin of a Thursday!..

Sorry... Sorry, I didn't mean to... Yes, yes of course. The law.'En-entitled to a - a slice of the cake.

Seven?.. 'Does not surface... after seven years can be legally... declared dead... Huh. I'll be past it by then...

All I can do is, is rent it?.. Oh, great. Strangers move in, I move out. Back to Flatsville. One rent cancelling out the other, just about... 'Never did fancy myself as a landlord.

Or, or I could stop the re-payments?.. I, I'm not with you?.. The, the Building Society re-possesses, sells. . . gives me a cut... eventually?.. Oh, dear… This, this is a lot messier than I thought.

Oh, yeah, something else I wanted to... What happens if, if I snuff it?.. She... she gets the lot?.. You mean, house, life insurance - everything?

Who - who's side are you on, anyway?.
Yes... Very well... I, I'll make a will...

Eh, I suppose Deserted Husbands' Allowance
would be out of the question?..
I - I don't qualify?..
No, I didn't suppose I would.
'Don't seem to qualify for much, really...

Well, anyway. Thank you for... Of course, yes - 'keep in
touch.

Caught, huh... Cornered... Nailed down… No divorce… No
way out... Cul de sac... No exit from Valium Valley...

So… that's the state o' play... so far.
'State. Free State. Irish Free State…
Free, my arse!
This comfortable, conservative Republic -
this, this plethora of gobshites and gombeen men -
does not sanction divorce.

'Turns a blind eye and a deaf ear
to just about any and every dubious practice,
double-think, in the book -
if you know someone who knows someone
you'll be all right, you'll be looked after -
but will not condone,
does not permit,
the final, legal imprimatur
to be stamped
on a marriage that has
irretrievably,
irremediably,
irrevocably
broken down...

Which leaves you, me oul' flower, in the shit...
Cheers.

There - there's always the Church?
Of course, yes! The sky pilots!
Bless me, Father, for I have sinned.
Annul me, Father, for I have foundered...

Good morning... Father. Fathers...

Thank you for seeing me so, so...

Well, as I explained in my letter,

detailed in your, your questionnaire...

I do, I understand that...

that annulment is not squaring the Pope -

sorry, I mean, not divorce by another name.

I do, I'm with you there...

Well, no... Suppose, suppose you tell me?..

Capable, incapable of undertaking the...

lifetime commitment... which marriage...

essentially is..?

Eh-hh... I'll have to take that one away with me,

mull over it...

Three... three, four years waiting... Long, isn't it?..

You must have one Helluva backlog -

either that or you're all scratch golfers!..

Sorry. Sorry, I didn't mean to...

Have, have your game of golf by all means –
and if you can get it at the right price,
more power to you!
Ha, ha! Sorry. 'Nerves, that's what that is...

What was that?.. 'No assurance my, my petition will be...
Well, yes, I can appreciate that...
Hmmm?.. Even, even if successful, no guarantee
I would be allowed to, to marry should I so wish...
'Would require the express permission of the,
the Ordinary of the Diocese...
You, you mean the Bishop?.. I see.
Fine. Well, we'll - as the man says –
we'll jump that one when we come to it...

A psychiatrist? No, of course not. By all means -
if you think it would, would help my case...
A lay expert in her specialised field?..
Yes, right, the very thing. You set it up and I'll
be there. Oh, without fail...

Pheeeew. .. 'Not easy... And not easy for them -
to, to go over all that. 'Doing their best...

Oh, I did - as I was leaving - I thanked them for,
for sifting through the, the rubbish
that is my life to date...
Celibacy, huh?.. Welcome to the club...

I might meet someone!.. 'might. 'Never know…
More fish in the sea than ever came out of it...

Hello, luv. Would you like to move in with me?
'Not a bad bit of a pad and the neighbours
would get used to you in jig time...
Ah, sure, in this day and age, what the hell!
I'd say for most of them you'd be a welcome relief -
from the monotony of the straight and narrow,
if you follow me...

Well, there's me. 'Have my own ways...
'bit of an odd ball, to be honest
but if you don't try to change me
you'll find I'm easy enough to...

Then there's Jenny. Ah, God, what can I say?!
You'd beg the earth with her!..
And she'd take a shine to you, I know she would,
if you went about it the right way...

Hmmm?.. Oh, my ex... Well, yes, she could come back, I
suppose... I mean, if things don't work out and she, she has
nowhere to go... I'd have to admit that...

Sorry?.. Well, no. Not really. You, you wouldn't have any
legal rights - if, if that's what you mean...

Hmmm?. Prospects?.. Well, not great, to be honest.
If, if we were to open a joint account in a Bank,
it would be about as close as you'd get to, to security...

Look, have a think about it, all right?.. Of course, yes,
you have your own family to consider.
'Parents, good living, respectable. . .
They, they'd find me hard to swallow?.. Indeed...

Hmmm?.. You, you'll ring me... You will, will you?..
Same time?.. At the same time, I, I'm
not getting any younger - know what I mean?..

What to do with her things?..
Clothes, bits and pieces, knick knacks?..
Remnants?.. Ha! Remnants...
So?.. Vincent de Paul... Sale o' Work?..
There's always the tip...
A skip, some night... dimlit street.

Hello, yeah?.. P J!.. Ah, very good of you...
Oh, I was in luck, that's all:
a contact gave me a number and that led me to...

Yeah, I saw the prints. Tim got some great shots...
Centre page spread, why not?.. Lead?.. Ah, game ball!..
Oh, it will… run and run... Ha. Try and stop me...
I've got one or two angles I want to...
Would you believe, crack of dawn?!.

Ah, not so bad... 'could be worse...
The wee one is a bit of a problem but I'm managing.
So far, so good...

And look, P.J… I, I just want you to know...
'Not easy to talk in the office...
I, I do appreciate all you...
'Make it up to you, that's for sure...
Good night, P.J… God bless...

One of the best... Gave me time off when I had to hurry here,
rush there, make it elsewhere...

And tomorrow, a shrink…

Ah, feck you, Emma! Feck you from a height!

It's you should be going - not me..

Hello, good afternoon... Nice to meet you.

Oh-hh. No couch?.. I always thought...

'Sit, sit anywhere?..

Well, I'll settle for a chair if it's all the same to you!

Ha, ha. Sorry. Sorry, you mustn't mind me.

I, I'm a bit jumpy - 'never been to a...

Hmmm?.. Relax?.. Yes, of course. 'Course I will...

'Mind if I smoke?.. Oh... Oh, well no...

It doesn't matter, I'll manage... I can always - ha, ha –

suck my - ha, ha, y'know - my thumb! Ha, ha...

How, how do y'mean, interests?..

Well, no. Green fingers, no.

Oh, I cut the grass before it turns into a meadow

but that's about it.

Well, whatever's there. Flowers, shrubs.
If it grows, it grows. If not, too bad...

The fella that sold us the house,
he planted a few bits and pieces.
'Doing all right as, as far as I know... No, him.
The magnolia died... Ha, ha. Got you, huh?..
On a - ha, ha - a technicality! Sorry.

Well... Golf. Golf for sure. Number One... Ah, total.
On the telly, the carpet in the front room, out the back.
And when I tee off - ah, sure, where would you be going?!.
Though I don't seem to be able to score around the greens –
feck it, anyhow... Sorry.

There, there was a time I had a go at the theatre...
Ah, but I gave up.
I mean, by the time you got in and parked and settled,
then home again - sure the night was gone.

And the year we had a Summer I went for a swim. Or two.
'Bloody cold, the sea. I, I had to have a brandy, after.

Mmmm... You're going back a bit, now...
Well, yes. Yes, as a matter of fact.
I was. Into plays and all like that
at school...
And the brothers knew it.

One, one day Brother O'Toole walked in -
I was in Fifth Year, taking it easy -
and called me out.
I was sure I was in for it
but it wasn't that at all.

There was this group of players
coming to the town
and they wanted a lad that'd be interested
for crowd scenes and walk-ons.
Ha! I only leapt at it!

The Monday evening I was round to the hall
and shown into the presence:
God he was tall!
Loch of blonde hair, blue eyes and a boom of a voice:
Anew MacMaster.

Not that I ever got talking to him.

He was way above me.

Just stood there, 'me mouth open...

They were opening with Romeo and Juliet.

When the time came I was led round and up on the stage,

a sword put in me hand.

'Crowded. This fella facing me.

"What do I do?" says I.

"When the curtain goes up," says he, "start fighting..."

Oh, well you may smile!

But it was, like,

a kick-start to a wondrous season!

I was a soldier in MacBeth,

a mariner in Othello,

another citizen in

the Merchant of Venice,

one of the chorus in Oedipus Rex –

as near to him as I am to you now –

ah, nearer -

when he came on again at the end,

the eyes out of his head!..

Ah, I didn't half get a fright...

Towards the end of the run
Mac said they were going on a tour to Australia
and would I like to come?
Ah, like that. Australia...

But the father and the mother said no,
get your Leaving first,
you won't get anywhere without your Leaving.

So off they went and I bent over the handle bars
into another winter of east winds and short days
and everything through Irish.
Am here ever since...

All my life I followed the safe way:
You have to be more than a bit mad
to take a chance, go out on a limb,
step off the end of the pier...
It's something I'm meaning to share
with Jenny when she gets a bit older...

'Few years ago, I read in the paper
where he died. Mac.
End of Act One, huh?

They're very lucky to have him:
He'll do Shakespeare for God Almighty
and all his angels and saints for saecula...

The Monday after they were gone
I went round to the Library above and took out
The Merchant of Venice.
"Many a time and oft on the Rialto..."
I kept at it until I had it be heart.

Though I didn't know it at the time
it was a way of trying to stretch to the
far ends of the earth, keep him in mind...

I could do a fair take on of him
as Shylock. I could.
'Said it to some of the local group once
but they said
I wouldn't have been right for it.
I would have been.
I know I would have been...

Here, why am I telling you all this?!
'Helps you to..? All part of the process...
'Case history... I see, yeah...

Hmmm… Now you're digging deeper still…
You'll have me back in the womb next!

Well… looking back now…
I, I lived a lot in my head, as a lad.
Like, I was the last in the –
brothers and sisters well ahead of me.
They were stretching their wings
while I was still in the nest –
if y'know what I mean…

I didn't know them. Not really…
And my Dad was away a lot and my mother
working the pub, trying to make ends meet.
So I - I turned into a world of me own…

Well, like, you won't believe this
but I used to write letters.
To, to the Little Flower. God's truth…
Saint Teresa of, of Lisieux.

'Nearly every night. Two, three pages.
With the fountain pen I got for Christmas.
No matter how cold it was in that bedroom.

And I'd leave them folded under her statue
on the tallboy before I'd get under the blankets…

God only knows what became of them.
Dumped, I suppose, like a lot of other stuff
when the family home was sold off…

And there's a thing: whenever I go into a Church now
she's nearly always there to one side or another,
standing with the bunch of roses,
looking at me…

And I think, maybe, she might just get me into Heaven
by a side door when – when the time comes…

All right? Okay? So… when do you think
I should start writing me memoirs?..

What? Sorry?.. Have, have a look at these cards...
Hmmm… Not playing cards, that's for sure.
Just blobs and smears of black ink… different shapes and -
Bit of a mish-mash, if you ask me...

You, you want me to - ha, ha - look at each in turn and - ha,
ha -
tell, tell you whatever comes - ha, ha - comes into my
head?!...
Sorry. I will, will take it seriously... Ha, ha. Sorry.

All right. All right, then... Here we go.
Any - anything for an annulment...

Eh-hhh... Lunar surface... How about that for openers?

Eh-hhh... Alien. Aliens...

Next... eh-hhh... Hiroshima...

Eh-hhh... Amazon...

This one... Ragdoll.

Oh, no, sorry... Eh-hh... Straw man.

I mean - what am I at? –
scarecrow...

Mmmmm... Space capsule - rocket...

Eh-hhhh... Car crash - multiple pile-up...

Oh. 'That all?.. For now, anyway?..
Thanks be to Jay - ! Eh, I can't say I'm sorry –
to be honest with you...

You, you'll send your report on to the Tribunal?..
I see... Well, then...

'Bet I had you fooled there for a minute:
you thought I was going to say Santa, Santa Claus -
but there really wasn't enough grey for a beard,
now was there?..

If, if I think of anything else that'd be useful
I can always write it out, post it in?
Well, we'll see. Now that you have me going.
Maybe after a night's sleep...

'Just as well it wasn't you, Emma...
you wouldn't have gone the distance...

Down Memory Lane, huh?..
Sifting... trawling... culling... stirring...
Browsing buried archives...
There. All the time.
Somewhere in the shadows of my mind...

Oh, she's good at her job, this lady.

A dab hand at turning locks,

drawing back curtains,

bringing me along forgotten corridors,

back down the years...

PENNY FOR YOR TRAVELS

Sunday afternoon… long-ago Winter...
My father was taking Sandy for a walk
and would I like to come?..

Would I!..

Out the North road with our
one-year-old, golden cocker...
The countryside still,
frosted, crunching underfoot.
A listless sun in a fading sky...

Gulls on the wing, inland from a barren seascape:
wheeling... screaming... foraging.
And in the distant, grotesque trees,
cacophonous crows...

Sandy soon off the lead...
sniffing, searching, darting,
exploring, checking...

*Here Sandy! Here! Come on, boy!.. Sandy?.. Sandy!.. That a
fella!*
That's the good dog!

My feet numb in boots that needed mending.
Still awkward in my first pair of long trousers.
At Dad's side, keeping up…
Bumping, nudging, jigging… chatter-boxing...

Him listening, nodding, musing...

Smoking... And again, smoking -

as if, somehow, the glow of a Sweet Afton

could warm him, ward off the insidious chill...

Oriel Park on Sunday, eh Dad?..

Dundalk at home to Shelbourne and if they come up against

Shamrock Rovers in the Final would I be able to go up to

Dublin with the lads on the train to cheer them on?..

God, if we won!?.. And why wouldn't we?!

With Joey Donnelly out on his own at centre forward

and Tizard the greatest goalie EVER?!

And I'd say I'll be picked for the Junior League

before much longer, the way I'm coming on...

And I'm praying to God I get a football for me birthday...

Isn't it funny the way I kick with my left and write with the

other?

And didn't Brother O'Toole catch some of the lads at the back whisperin' and gigglin' when he made a sudden turn from the blackboard? You shoulda seen his face - Don MacDonagh is on his last warning...

And if I get a scholarship from the Gaelic League I'll be off to Rannafast in the Summer... Or I might be going, anyway – mightn't I not?..

And how long more do y'think Tom will be in the Sanitorium?
And will we be going back up to Dun Laoghaire to see him again soon?
Brother Kennedy was saying it's very unusual the number in his class that got it...

And is it true, Dad, there's no cure?
And is that why he wants to go all the way to Arizona - because the air out there is that dry he'd be back on his feet in no time?..

And is it true, Dad, when I was born, Tom came in to have a look at me and said to Mammy in the bed –

"I'm not the pet anymore..."

And was I a big surprise, Daddy? Because one day there not so long ago I heard Maggie Carney saying to Mammy - "Where did you get him at all, at all, at your age, Missus?"

And you should see their faces when they have to mind me! Mickey says I'm a terrible nuisance and Rita I'm a spoilt brat and Monica is sure I tell on her and I'm afraid of me life of Charlie...

Sure I know the McKennas better - see more of the MacEnteggarts - than I do my own...

And if Mickey gets called to Dublin for the Junior X will I be able to move into his room?..

Well, he can get his own Brylcream - 'not be whippin' mine.

*D'y'know, 'not wantin' to get him into trouble, I wonder is
he a Pioneer a tall any more?.. I'm nearly sure I got a whiff
off him the other night when he came in from the Hop out at
the Rock...*

*And what do you think of Monica not being able to get a job
up the North because she doesn't kick with the right foot?..
'Won't stop her laughing and smiling and telling jokes - I bet
you any money...*

*And how much do you think Charlie gets for playing the
fiddle in the band - when he's not sweltering over the
correspondence course in Accountancy?..*

*He brought it out there one night we had visitors - and do
y'know what I'm goin' to tell you?- his Blue Lagoon was as
good as anything you'd get round in the Pavilion...*

*Oh, and Jimmy O Dea is coming next week - a picture first
and then the stage show...*

---

*And Donny McCann is standing some of us in Maloccas –
soon, so he says. It was his birthday there one day last week -
it'll be egg and chips and we'll end up chipping in, wait till
you see...*

*And I haven't made up my mind yet what I'm going to be
when I grow up but it'll very likely be Bursar on a big liner...*

*Or mebbe an actor - but I'd be afraid I'd forget some o' the
lines... Anyway, me teeth aren't great and the dentist says
that Dutch chocolate after the War was a killer...*

*Jimmy McMahon gave out free passes to the Magnet last
week and do y'know how many times I saw The Hunchback
of Notre Dame? Two first houses and two matinees...*

*And some of us, after, went round the Demesne to the big tree
and Nicky Hardy had a rope and I did the Hunchback for
them and they all said I was as good as your man any day...*

*And to tell you the truth, Dad, I know it's a lovely piano but
I'd sooner be out with the lads and I dread Missus Glass
going over me scales with me and The Robin's Return gives
me the pip - there's times I could drown him, the same robin!*

And anyway, Mister Van Dessel says I'm not too musical and that I'll never be the singer me brother Mickey is and that mebbe I'd be better off serving Mass, not singing at it...

And he should know because he's from Belgium where they make all the organs and he has a tuning fork and can read music the way I read the Champion or the Hotspur...

And Dad, Dad! Wait'll I tell you!

Didn't Missus Glass call to the door one rainy day there last week and me upstairs in front of the big mirror, practicing me draw and shooting straight from the hip just like Hopalong Cassidy.

And what do y'know, doesn't Mammy let her in and there she is in the hall, a wee fat wan with three chins and the glasses perched on a button nose. And before I know where I am wasn't Mammy calling up to me -

John? Missus Bottle is here!..

Oh, well you may laugh...

And the penny never dropped – honest to God! 'Goes back into the pub, not a feather out of her, leaving me to drag me heels over the linoleum and down the stairs to face the music... Trying to keep a straight face, pass it over, not let on... And Missus Glass standing on the mat with a face on her like a wet Democrat...

And Brother Maloney says sixteen nine naught, the Battle of the Boyne was fought - and that that's the way to remember that... And we have a new name on him now and if he ever finds out it'll be the leather...

And Brother Rehill has me reading A Tale of Two Cities and I'm not taking in half of it and can't see meself ever getting to the end...

And there's a Ceili and Old Time in the Hall on Sunday night and will Mammy let me go, I wonder?.. And why does she not want me going round the Back o' the Wall at night?.. Other lads are let...

And she always gets a laugh out of Wassey with the Hair Lip and Rummy Dumb Dumb... And why does she say Uncle Peatie's not like another?..

And d'you know what she said to Missus Melber the other day? "Ah, there y'are, Mam, with your two feet the one length!.." Honest to God... To Missus Melber!?..

And why does she say Mister Duffner is only a runner - when she knows right well he's lived in Seatown for years and years?..

And Dad, Dad! This'll give you a laugh! Do y'know what she was sayin' to Sandy the other day when I walked into the kitchen?.. "Ah-hh, the one wee paw... and the two wee paws!.."

To Sandy?.. You should have seen him looking up at her!..

And guess what, Dad! Well, mebbe you know already but I only found out there lately - one o' the men Mammy lets into our pub of a Sunday writes plays... Yeah, plays!

I heard her tellin' Fanny Clinton one day I was passin' the
snug... Be the name of Carroll... Paul Vincent... Vincent I
took for me Confirmation so I suppose we have that much in
common... And his plays are on in Dublin and Glasgow and
New York, even.

New York!

And Fanny was sayin' Canon Toal takes a poor view -
whatever's in them... So didn't I have a peep for myself
through the keyhole in our hallway last Sunday. . . Sittin'
there he was at the back o' the pub with two or three of his
friends... them talkin' and jokin' and laughin'...

Mammy keepin' her distance...

And honest to God, Dad, he's just like another.
I mean, you'd never think to look at him he writes PLAYS!..

And what did I do but didn't I go out the kitchen door to the
yard when Mammy was lettin' them out the wicket gate - I
don't think they were bona fide at all - hopin' that he'd stop
and say Hello...

But he just gave me a quick look and a wee smile and kept goin'...

Still, I can always say I saw him... Paul Vincent Carroll... That atself... as near to him as I am to you now - eh, Dad?..

And what do you think of Rita not havin' to wear glasses any more? Her new boss made her take them off, step into the street and read the time on Russell's clock. And she did and she could and that was that...
And her that had them on all during the Shorthand and Typing course...

Well, glasses or no glasses, she wasn't long about gettin' off her mark with the high stepper that started work there lately with the County Council...

So Mammy was tellin' Maggie Carney the other day when they were puttin' the sheets through the mangle. And Maggie was tellin' Mammy it's a very strong line altogether...

She knows someone that was sittin' beside them in the back row of the Adelphi the other night at the second house... It was no good of a picture so they didn't miss much...

Anyway, we'll be able to hear what he sounds like on the wireless some Sunday night soon –

Question Time is comin' to the Town Hall and I heard Mickey sayin' your man is down for it on account o' havin' some class of a degree so we'll know what he's made of when he comes up against Joe Linnane - eh, Dad?..

Oh, and one night there during the week when you were away, didn't I walk into the front room thinking it was empty. And what do y'know, Mammy and Maggie sittin' behind the lace curtains at one of the windows looking down at the crowds going past in Park Street and across at the neighbours...

And when I switched on the light they jumped up and you'd swear I was after committin' a mortal sin the way they went for me! And Mammy said she'd slaughter me with the dish cloth when she got me down to the kitchen...
And why wouldn't I switch on the light - wasn't it dark?..

*And why does she sometimes say to Maggie - when the mood
takes her - "Yoo hoo! You ould doll ya!"
Or maybe another time, out of the blue -
"Mind the dresser, Brigid!.."*

*And is it the end of the crowds coming down on the trains
from Belfast - or will there be more fights and rows and
broken glass in Anne Street?
And the barriers nearly giving way on Platform One?..*

*And will the American soldiers ever be back down from the
North with chewing gum and Lucky Strikes and Camels and
money to burn?..*

'Walkin' Clanbrassil Street as if they owned it.

*And will I ever hear, I wonder, from the pilot in the eight Air
Corps who promised to bring me out to California? And
would I be let go, do y'think, if he sent the fare?. .
Or was he only pullin' me leg?..*

*Still, there's great readin' in the Saturday Evening Posts he
gave me. Well for him that gets it every week... I like the
front covers and the cartoons the best...*

So that's what its like in America, huh? Just goes to show - you can't believe everythin' you see at the pictures, eh Dad.

And a priest from the Redemptorists gave us the School Retreat not so long ago and Frank Muldoon hasn't cursed since and Gerry Crosby broke it off with Philomena Farrell...

And I went to him for confession and it was behind a screen in a classroom in the Primary... And I was afraid of me life but he wasn't the same a tall as when we were all together in the Hall and he was telling us from the stage that it only took one mortal sin...

So I was a new pin coming away... Though I thought my turn would never come - the lad before me was in with him for ages, whatever was going on...

And the Legion of Mary meeting is tomorrow night round the Ramparts... And if I'm put down again for the Kiosk at St. Patrick's at the early Masses I'll have to wind the big alarm clock.

The Messenger and the Catholic Fireside are my favourites...

And Dad, Dad! Can we go swimming again like we did last
year when I get my summer holidays?!.

I was already there!..
A sudden flash of memory breaking through
a bank of ice-cold clouds...

A fairy-wand recall
of blue skies and clear water
and boats at anchor
lapped by a warm wind.
Ah! The pier at Gyles' Quay:
a finger-and-thumb extension
of the Cooley mountains,
reaching into the Irish Sea...

Tanned youngsters and browning, browsing elders.
Carefree girls and circumspect women.
Talk and laughter,
swimming and diving…

In off the steps or braver still,

a plunge from the harbour wall...

Splash... and splash again...

Towel down... dry out...

Egg and onion and tomato sandwiches...

Did flasked tea ever taste so good?..

I was only a nipper when Dad

took me in out of my depth...

on his back,

my arms around his neck,

holding on for dear life...

Oh, Dad, hold me! Oh, it's deep, Dad!.. And here's another wave! I'm slippin', Dad! Dad, don't let me go – Dad!..

No fear... And no fear of the sea from that day to this.

Oh, but he was a strong swimmer!

Out and around... then back to the pier,

the lower steps green-mossed at ebb tide.

'Faded as swiftly as it had sprung to mind...
and I was back on the side
of a pot-holed road
that meandered north west
to Monaghan and the Black North...

We will - won't we, Dad?..

It was there in my voice - a growing apprehension
that my dreams of Summer would not come true,
the fear that I would lose my Dad to another, alien Sport...

That's if the golf doesn't take over altogether...

Said I, ruefully - Indeed, tauntingly -
Almost, if not quite, resentfully.
Off golfing... Again? Again!..

A round with Walter Carroll, no less.
Or Mister Ward from the Hibernian bank.
Or Jimmy Cassidy, the square-set,
smooth-swinging, resident Pro...

And did they smile wryly the day he crossed
into the semi-rough to pluck Spring grass
and offer it to a new-born lamb?..

Nor did I witness his hour of triumph:
striding out... head high...
down the eighteenth fairway...
not quite believing it...
on his way to the Captain's Prize.

*"Well, would you credit that!? Harry in the Winner's
Enclosure!*
Away all week, then goes out and plays a blinder!..
Bates all! He's some operator, no doubt...
Have to hand it to him!..
*Ah, indeed, you do know him! Sure, everyone knows
Harry!.."*

That was the year, Dad! That was the year!
*I don't know much about it - to tell you the truth, I think
it's a sissy's game - but still, it was a great win!*

Sissy's game?.. How little I knew!
God knows he did his best to ween me:
a few clubs, the occasional lesson,
bringing me out and about,
coaching, coaxing, encouraging...

But I didn't take to it, wouldn't bite, dug in,
went against him, went with the lads,
settled for hanging around the Square...

'Stood on the footpath outside our pub
beside the pipe-smoking,
hard-spitting veterans of the Great War
as he cycled off,
clubs strung across his back,
undaunted by the petrol rationing,
ignoring the jibes and jeers and taunts
of the waifs and wantons in Hill Street...

Dad?.. Can we go home now, Dad?.. I'm frozen...

Said I... easing a cold hand
into a pocket of his overcoat...

Here, boy! Here, Sandy!.. Come on, fella!.. Sandy?!.. Ah, that a boy!..

Back into town, downhill...

Passing traffic: Anglias and Austins,
Standards and Morris Minors...
The occasional pony and trap.

By the Railway Station,
the terraced, red-bricked houses
forming a crescent
above and around and about
the grey Dominican Church...

Paying scant attention
to the man approaching
on the other side of the road,
walking four greyhounds on the lead...

Only sensing danger as they
strained forward,
sighting, targeting
the unsuspecting spaniel
that was padding towards them
sniffing, scenting,
tail-wagging...

Sandy ,no! Don't, don't Sandy! Here boy, here! Come to me!
Oh, God, no - Sandy!..

So sudden! Jesus, they engulfed him,
went for his belly as he rolled over,
whimpering.

I can still hear
his frantic cries as they tore him -
relentless onslaught...

'Stood riveted as Daddy tried to fight them off,
the handler pull them back...

And then, then it was over...
Dad carrying the pup in his arms -
paws limp, dark eyes anguished -
as we hurried the rest of the way home:

To the basket by the fire
in the front room,
the sheets soon bloodied,
the 'phone call to the vet,
the many stitches...
Injections that would stave off
for a night's vigil
the inevitable, final sorrow.

A mere twelve months before
I had lifted and held him
for the very first time:
warm, trembling, liquid-eyed, moist-nosed.

Sandy... Oh dear, dear... Poor Sandy...

'Died the next day. In his sleep.

'Heart just stopped.

On his side, under the bay window,

in the bed we had made up for him

the night before...

And Dad blinking at a dead fireplace.

Not wanting us to see him,

fumbling a handkerchief to his face.

Trying to conceal what we already knew -

that he was a quiet, wee man... Big Softie...

Little did I know, then, that all too soon

there would be another -

far more harrowing - winter:

him in pain,

confined to the room

at the top of the stairs,

bed-ridden.

I'll just take your tray, Dad... Oh?.. 'Mebbe gave you too much?.. Will, will I make you a fresh drop?..

Dad?.. Dad, there's something I want to... 'On the tip o' me tongue for... Dad, I... Look, even when you shot me down, gave out stink... And the few times you belted me around the place, I... I still loved you... No matter what... I love you, Dad...

But I didn't, did I?.. Just gentled the tray out and closed the door on another chapter of What Might Have Been...

'Not easy... not easy when you're sixteen going on ten…
Or thirty six going on twelve... to say... say straight up -

And I suppose, Dad... looking back... I... I suppose I deserved it - the beating you gave me when I reared up... Though I thought at the time you were unfair... Oh very, to tell you the truth... 'Still do... deep down… to be honest...

But look, Dad... if I could just say... without you flyin' off the handle... If, if I am - and I suppose you're right - a, a spoilt brat then, then was it all my fault?.. I mean, who - who spoilt me in the, the first place?..

Dad?.. You don't mind me sayin' that, Dad?.. Dad?.. God,
there's a hundred things I want to... want to... but I...

Do, do you see what I'm tryin' to?.. I mean, you were away
all week, nearly every... and Mammy below in the pub tryin'
to make ends meet... And when you came home you were only
in and you were away again - more often than not...

So I, I went next door or down the street...
out and about with the lads.
Cowboys and Indians down the Demesne -
'Come out with your hands up!'

Climbin' trees, robbin' nests, blowin' eggs...
Or coggin' from Gerry Corr's home work...
Or gettin' over the wall into Hardy's orchard...
Or buyin' five Woodbines before we sneaked into the pit
at the Oriel by the side door...

And I mitched from school, Dad. I did...
The odd day... Meself an' Hughie Lennon...
'Spent most of it out down the Harbour... under the bridge...
with now and again... the train to Greenore passin' over.

Or dossing and smoking in the Snooker Hall...
'Scribbled a note to Brother O'Toole the next mornin',
forged your name to it...
Watched, shakin', as he tucked it away in a pocket
of his soutane to read after, mebbe... mebbe not?..

And when the lads got at me one night down a side street
to kiss Doreen Deery, I did. 'Didn't really want to -
she's not much to look at - but I did...
Just to show... to show them that... Oh, I dunno...
I always fell in with them. Always. No matter what...

And when Mickey or Monica was sent out to call me in it was
to go to bed and shut me eyes and ears and dream of what it
would be like away, away - mebbe even as far as
California...

What I might have said...
And how would he have responded?..

Man to boy?.. Man to man?
Voices whispering in the stillness
of a sick-room...
His eyes on mine as he lay, pillowed.

As the days and the nights, the weeks and the months
went by the malignancy slowly spread.
My father on the rack,
relieved, decreasingly, by morphine...

Dad?.. Dad?.. It's me, John... I brought you up a glass o'
water...
Will you not try and... Dad?.. 'Even a drop?.. Daddy?..

The occasional visitor - relative, friend -
well meaning but draining him further, for all that.

The many who chose to stay away,
remember him as he was,
'send, instead, a message of concern,
a promise of prayers, Novenas,
an assurance of Masses...

And further afield still,
around the Province and beyond the Pale,
his many customers and contacts
would grieve his passing
when they read the notice
in the daily papers…

And won't you take me with you, Dad, like before - on some
of your trips - when I get me holidays?.. Away Monday to
Friday! Yipee!..

Me packed and washed and shining,
warm and secure and proud as Punch,
beside him in the Morris Minor,
chugging along at forty,
knowing he'd get us there and home again, safely...

Ah, the week he took me on the Cavan run!!

And that other time to Wicklow!
Staying, staying in hotels!.. HOTELS!..

From Arklow to Coothill,
Avoca to Virginia,
Ballyhaise to Enniskerry,
Shercock to Wooden Bridge…

And the Manageress with a soft spot for me
and whatever's on the menu
and me ordering and a waitress
putting it in front of me
on a white cloth...
Then coming back after another while to ask -

Would yis like another loch o' chips?..

And Dad whispering I was to put the knife
and fork together in the middle of the plate
when I was finished…

Why, I don't know... None of us ever had to do it at home...

And the other travellers
in the Commercial Room
swapping yarns, joking,
regaled by Daddy's latest!
Me listening... open-mouthed...

*'This fella in a pub, drinking pints... Ah, well on... After a
while he goes out the back... There's a tap running in the
yard and he thinks it's himself - stands there all night!..'*

Up and about the next morning,
order-book in hand... moving from one
point of sale to the next...
A Teetotaler all his life,
brightening every pub and hostelry
he walked into,
receiving a warm welcome
wherever he went... My father.

Checking out, noting down, writing up...
So many dozens of this, crates of that,
siphons of the other...

Lemonade and Mi Wadi,
Stone Beer and Orange Squash…
Smooth strokes with a fountain pen,
Impeccable penmanship…

Dad? Is that the pitch where the Cavan team practises?
Really, Dad?.. Brother Staunton says they're bound to win
the All-Ireland again this year, they're that good…

And Dad! If we come back this evening, Dad, we might see
John Joe O'Reilly going up for a ball? Mightn't we not?..
Charlie says he's the best centre half-back ever!..

Then away to another townsland:
more wooden counters
and sawdust and general groceries -

Thanks very much for the Bull's Eyes, Missus…

Dad singing away, betimes, as we bowled along:

'Mersey dotes and dosey dotes and little lambs eat ivy –
Kids eat ivy, too - wouldn't you?..'

Or smiling as we passed the County Council workers
leaning on their shovels – chancing his wee bit of Irish:

'Fir ag obair...'

Or tellin' me one of his tall ones:

There were three bears - Daddy Bear, Mammy Bear and
Baby Bear.
And they went asleep for the winter in this cave - same as
every year. Only this time they overslept it and when they
woke up it was the middle of Summer and they were in the
wrong part of the world, altogether!..

And they began to swelter in their fur coats...

So Mammy Bear, the practical one, said Come on, we'll go
down to the village in Fur-n-Feather Land and get three big
blocks of ice and sit up on them – and that'll cool us off...

So they did. 'Went down and got these three big blocks of ice
and sat on them... And in no time a tall they were grand and
cool...
Then, to pass the time, Daddy Bear said - 'I have a tale to
tell...' And Mammy Bear said, 'I have a tale to tell, too...'
And little Baby Bear, he stuck his nose up in the air and he
said - 'My tale is told...'

Oh, Dad! Where do you get them?!..

And when I went quiet for a while he took his eyes
off the road to search mine: blue on blue...

'Eh, John!.. A penny for your thoughts!..'

If he only knew! So much I wanted to ask,
find out about him:

Dad? Dad, is it true you only ever drank the odd bottle of
cider?.. And that you put up the pin when you were
nineteen?..

And were you really a wireless operator, Dad? And did you
go round the world on a ship?.. And write to Mammy from
every port?.. And has she still your letters in that trunk none
of us can get into?.. And is it true you were dead lonely?..
But how can you be lonely, Dad, in Greece - or Gibralta?..

And that when you came home and went for that interview in
Belfast - a better job on a bigger ship – the other fella got it
because you didn't know the Free Mason handshake?..

But I didn't, did I? Just sat there, quietly,
contentedly, as he turned the wheel,
headed North West to the coast…
Up and across to wondrous Donegal:
majestic mountains framed by an azure sky...

Oh, look Dad, look! Is that the Atlantic? The Atlantic! I can
wish!..

A sprint across golden sand to sea's edge
and the dull sound of lazy breakers...

Come on, Daddy! This is great!..

And when a sudden, treacherous wave

caught me unawares,

bowled me over,

pinned me down,

he was there to pull me up

and out of the swirling,

foaming, sea-weeded swell...

Oh, Dad. I was never as scared... 'Under before I could
catch me breath...

And that other time at Wicklow's Courtown

when I raced into the sea not knowing

there was a sand shelf and a sudden drop -

he was on hand, reaching for me, as I

struggled to the surface –

gasping... winded.

Oh, Dad!.. Got such a fright!.. Didn't know where I was...

There for me. Always. Saving. Assuring. Re-assuring...

And then… then there were the Day Trips!
The Home Run!..
A sweep across the hinterland:
Winding, country roads...
hedge-rowed, alive with bird song...

Channonrock of the strawberry beds,
Mullacrew of the many orchards,
heavy with autumnal fruit...
Inishkeen of the Sunburst Oats.

Or left at Castlebellingham
and out the coast road to Annagasson:
Ginger ale and a bun in Clinton's pub,
fishermen talkin' tides and salmon…

Then on by Dunany Point and Salterstown
To Clogher Head…

'Time for a quick dip, Dad, off the pier?!..

Or out by Ravensdale and Riverstown

to Carlingford of the Norman castles.

Lemonade and biscuits in O'Hare's pub,
me on a high stool...
The Railway hotel in Greenore;
herrings and mash in O'Meath...

And Dad! Over there is the hostel where me and Michael
Flanagan stayed with An Oige ...

The sweep of the Lough across to the foot of the
Mourne Mountains... breath-taking.

How is it they're so different up the North, Dad?
'Looks all the same to me...

And can some of the old people around here still speak Irish,
Dad?.. You're not coddin' me?.. No, I never heard them
meself - but mebbe it's just that they're shy...

The return that evening across the Cooley range
along a twisting, winding road.
Sheep guarded by sentinels of rock
from an ancient Age.

The eventual drop to the main road...

This is the way we came, Dad, after the War. A few of us on
our bikes across the Border to Newry for the white bread....

And the police in the car with the loud speaker
cutting across our chatter -

Two abreast!..

Stopped and searched at the border:
An alien in uniform scarcely suppressing a sneer
when he came upon my Rosary beads...

Mammy says he musta been black...

The Cemetary on our left as we headed into town.
Sign of the Cross and a quiet prayer for kith and kin:
Granny who had had a long life and Tom,
athlete and scholarship winner,
downed in his prime by an unmentionable incurable...

Home soon, Dad! Ah, it was great!.. And won't you bring me
with you again before long?..

But there would be no next time...

Here we are, Dad! Journey's End!..

If he knew he was at the end of the road he never let on -

not to me, anyhow...

Long, harsh winter... Brief hours of weak daylight
giving way, all too soon, to inevitable night.
North east wind, prevailing,
showing no mercy, taking no prisoners...

And in the room at the top of the stairs,
the struggle for air... breath... life,
growing weaker by the hour...

In coma...

Then surfacing

to ask the shadows

at the end of the bed was it

Father MacAvoy that was

in with him earlier?

And was he due another injection

and could he have it now?.. NOW!

Sinking... Rallying...

And again, sinking...

Wasting... wasted.

Parting... departed.

Mammy kneeling, pressing his hands as his life ebbed.

Michael leaning against the door, head bowed.

'Sprinkle of holy water… urgent whispering…

Holy Mary, Mother of God… now and at the hour of our…

Oh, no!.. NO!.. Dad, no!

Leaving me stricken, stunned…

Oh, Dad... Jesus mercy, Mary help... My Dad...

...sundered.

PLAYBACK

John 1 v John 2:

Here, get a move on! You'll just about make it.

- What?

The Meeting.

- No!

Yes!

- I don't…

Want? Want! Which of them does? What one of them would
go if they didn't have to? Huh? Huh!
- Those faces. All that smoke.
Now look, get it into your thick skull, once and for all: it's a
life-line, your only hope this side of the grave; throw it away
and you won't be on bottled water much longer...
So be a man and move it: get there, walk in and take a place
- your place - among your own.
Yes, I do mean it: among - your - own...
It's a fellowship, damnit.
Support... Share... Concern... Help...
They don't need you but by God, do you need them!..
All you've done so far is put the cork back in the bottle,
right?
Take the hand of the one next to you - his, hers - and know
he's gone down the same road, she's been through a similar
mill... that nothing they could say to you, you to them, would
be from a different file...

Clasp... hold on... hang in there...
But not your head: there is no shame in forming such a
circle, being one of such a company, praying the prayer they
live - try to live - a day at a time:

God, grant us serenity...

———

- 'Never know who'd be there - mebbe someone that'd know me from somewhere...
So?.. Who'd get the bigger shock?

- And, and if I'm asked to... to?..
Say it.
- My, my name is...
Yes!
- 'Name is... My name is John -
'Can't hear you!
- I... l am...
Loud and clear!
- I, I am a... an -
Now!
- An... I am an...
And mean it!..

- Jenny. That's it, Jenny! I can't leave her on her own -
'Will be just fine, and well you know it. An hour, two at the most.
And you know how she wants you to go, the difference in you when you get back...
For her sake, then?..
- Jenny... Yes. Yes, for her –
Car keys?

- Hanging up.

Okay, then. Let's do it in the name o' God!..

Jenny!.. Jenny, I'm home!.. You up there, kiddo?..
Jenny?..

Hmmm…

Messages, eh… Messages…

Are you ever in?!.. Listen, I have us on the Time Sheet for Saturday - 11.08, all right?
It's the qualifier for the Captain's Prize so you'll have to play out of your skin. No messin', right?..
And will you for God's sake do something about that slice?!
Oh, and the Missus wants the car so is it all right if I go with you? Give us a bell to confirm, right?

Jeez, have I got news for you! And I mean NEWS. We're talking leak with a capital L, okay? Tonight, about ten, the usual place. I'll be in the lounge, corner table... 'Say no more.

———

186

Jenny... eh, this is Carl.
We eh, we met on Saturday night at the party in Carsons...
Eh, you might not remember...
I, I'm the one that spilt the drink over eh, David Jones.
An, an accident - honest - I, I'm as awkward...
Anyway, I was - was wondering if we could mebbe meet
sometime? Like for a coffee or, or y'know, whatever..?
I, eh... I'd love to see you again...
So, eh... will you... would you like to?..
I, I'm not on the phone at home but eh,
Orla has a number where I can be... Anyway...

Ena Costello here. Jenny, are you free on Friday night?
George and I are going to a dinner party so I'd need you
from about half seven.
Will you let me know as soon as you can, please? And sorry
about the short notice...

Dad Dearest... 'Have scoffed my supper. 'Couldn't wait.
Yours is in the top oven.
I'm here at Orla's - a bit of swotting.
And would you believe, coffee and a natter?
You have the number if you need me...
Two more papers, Dadsers – two more exams - and that's it!
The Leaving behind me for good!..
Dad, if a boy called Carl rings will you please tell him I'll be
home later? Please.
And please, Dad, won't you be nice to him?..
And not abrupt like you were with Benny Lawless when I was
fifteen...
Ah, you're an angel... And I'm trying to be... See ya, Pops...

Jenny?! Oh, love, I was hoping to get you in.
Why, oh why, my darling, won't you write to me?!
I've written to you twice, three times, in the last few weeks -
big, long letters - and nothing, not a line from you...
Why? What is it? Is anything the matter, my love?
How are you getting on with your father?..
You have no idea how much I fret.
So please, please, write to me. Even a card...
'Your birthday soon, my sweet,
and I was hoping, praying, that somehow we could –
oh, I'm going to be cut off -
Next year, Jenny, for your eighteenth!
I with you or you out here with me - us.
And I really do mean –

Huh... Hmmmm…

'Knows bloody well I'd check my calls.

Playing with me... Cat and mouse...

Same old game... Playing on my...

Ah, give over, Emma. Just give over…

What is it - eight, nine years?..

Still going strong, still in orbit?.. Hmmm?..

Or are you lurking just beyond the shadows

of what was once a home?..

waiting in the wings...

for me to, me to... What?..

188

Emit final, phlegmatic wheeze?..

'Remorseless decline into senility...

Gibbering retreat into hypothermia...

Or sudden, unsignalled, cardiac arrest?..

Insidious aneurysm... What?.. Which?..

While you continue in untroubled,

untouchable orbit,

surviving admirably well,

thank you very much,

against all the odds,

despite ominous

forewarnings and predictions of

doctors,

specialists,

counselors!

Emma, the original creaking door -

not so much somewhat open as not quite closed.

A trifle rusty, doubtless... rusting...

but hanging in there for all that... ajar...

Ha. I like it. Creaking Emma... ajar...

Re-entering… re-appearing…

in suitable, subdued, attire,

acknowledging the commiserations of

mourners,

sympathisers,

camp followers…

Upper lip pursed,

barely concealing a sense of ultimate triumph.

Poised…

ready to claim,

re-possess,

sign for,

take over,

receive on demand

anything, everything - whatever -

when the last of the clay has been shovelled.

Ha. Hang in there, honey. 'Could be a long haul!

Is anything the matter, my love?
How are you getting on with your father?..

Worried, are you?.. Fretful?..
'Feeling a bit insecure, maybe?..
Afraid of losing your one and only -
could that be it?..
Needing the bit of reassurance?..

Does, does she still love you?.. Hmmm...
She - she hasn't said so -
not in so many words -
not in my hearing -
but yes, I reckon… yes.
I'd be a fool to think otherwise.
You are, after all, her mother...

And here! Here's one for you!
She's you. Ah, ha. You.
She - is - you. Mark Two.
Jenny. Emma's Jenny...

The gesture, swing of the head,
sudden, flashing glance...
As long as she lives, so will you...

Me? Oh, I fertilised the egg, end of story.
The eyes are mine, the contours, the sallow skin.

But behind the eyes, beneath the skin,
the persona that grew and evolved was - alien...

As if - as if you had come back to haunt me.
'Never, ever shake you off...
And when she turns to look at me -
as is her wont -
it's as if you were paces away,
not light years...

Once, twice - too often -
standing in the half-light...
Jenny… her back to me...
your head grew out of her shoulders,
turned, swivelled - full tilt -
to stare at me.

And when I cried, Jesus!
Jenny jumped!
And how was I to tell her? -
how was I to tell her! -
that it was just a
sudden, flashing, waking nightmare?..

'Haunted by my own wife
out of her daughter
whom she possessed
from the very moment of conception.
Jenny...

Walking, talking, sitting, sleeping replica –
of you.
Even as a child agrowing,
when I called her for school of a morning -
shook her shoulder -
she opened her eyes and you looked at me...

Why, oh why, my darling, won't you write to me?!

Emma, huh. Restless, frenetic Emma...
Oh, now and again she makes contact:
the few lines, the odd phone call...
Clear as a bell, immediate, in my ear.
Or vague -
crackling static on a faulty line,
echoing distort on a poor connection...

What?.. What's that?.. Sorry, I can't..?
Oh, Jenny!.. Yes, yes she's fine… good...
- *good as can be expected...*

'Grown up now - *if she's ever to grow up...*
'Sitting her Leaving...
We'll know how she does before long.

Sorry?.. Oh, she is, doing nicely...
all things considered... What's that?..
How do I mean, *all things considered?..*
Well, you know yourself.

You know well yourself, woman dear:
one minute in your womb...
the next in your arms,
at your breast...
and then, and then…
I mean, she recovered remarkably well
for a nine-year-old - hit by an express train...

Your pride and joy was she not?..
'Apple of your eye.
'Went everywhere with you.
Her hand in yours, trusting.

Down the village... main street...
gliding past the shops,
the park, the railway station:
a swan and her signet...

No word of warning, explanation... nothing.
Just - take-off.
How you were able to, to...

'Still... good of you to ring,
nice of you to enquire.
Indicates concern,
demonstrates devotion,
signals conscientiousness -
however ephemeral, transient, passing...

'Not easy to respond on the phone -
get beyond the stock cliche,
transcend the palpable platitude.

Great... fine... doing very well...
Not to worry... No problem...

'Not easy... to go for the jugular
if, if it's a bad line...
or she's suddenly hard of hearing or,
or she doesn't really want to know...

So... Can you hear me out there? *Over.*
Now? Are you receiving me? *Over.*
Loud and clear? *Over...* Good. Fine.
You were asking about Jenny?..
Well, of course, let me fill you in:

I reckon, suspect, you still see her as the fledgling
you left behind when you flew the nest long since...
your memories of her crystallised, static...
because, 'cause that's the way you'd like it to be -
would I be right?..

Well... you may be suspended in time and space -
for all I know - but not she, not our Jenny!
She's grown now, starting to stretch her wings...
'Can't see her settling. Not here. Not in this...

Some day, some day you'll maybe meet.
Some showdown that will be:
the ageing maverick and the matured offspring.
Ha! What I wouldn't give to be a fly on the wall!
Your best bet might be to dock in outer space,
batten down the hatches...

Will you have your friend along?
For support, like.
Y'know, the bird you're shacked up with -
What do y'mean, susschh?!

Of course she knows! Has done for -
oh, you'd be surprised how long!..
So don't go on about *Just good friends.*
No bullshit, if you don't mind!
It won't cut ice, she won't wear it!

Look, it was a big buzz when you took off,
the whole place had it!
I didn't know where to look...
'Sick and tired - oh, nauseated -
shovelling up the fall-out:
oodles and litres and kilos of - shit...

Hello, yeah?.. Sorry?.. Who?..

Oh, you're the fella was ringing earlier?.. Yeah, right...

No - but she should be in fairly soon... Eh-hh...

No, look, lad: to my certain knowledge she's not leaving for

Australia first thing in the morning, right?..

So relax, will you?.. Yeah, I'll tell her... Good luck.

There y'are, that's more of it.

Ah, well, we all have our problems.

Hmmm... 'Needs to blow his nose...

They'll be queuing up after another while.

Madly in love, huh?.. Ha...

Were we?.. Was I?.. I suppose so, yes.

Or was it just an emotional hype, straw in the wind?

Did you, Emma?.. Did we?.. Were we ever in love?..

Emma?.. Really?.. You me - I you?.. Love?..

Or were we simply wading through so much

sentimental slush, fending off reality?

'Embarked on a low tide of high passion -

an immature,

irresponsible,

wild, mad, frenetic fling?..

Love?.. Were we ever?.. Emma?.. Really?..
You won't, I reckon, want to admit it...
but you know as well as I do...
Let's face it… No?.. No?!.. No...

Oh, we had the equipment - ah, hadn't we! -
to bring children into the world.
But bring them up in the..? No, never!
We just hadn't the wherewithal...

There were two of us, Emma - two of us in it!
Unheeding bar loungers,
drifters who just didn't want to know -
'know what I mean?..

And along the way - slowly, surely -
we reduced our wee one -
starry-eyed, frolicsome, vivacious Jenny -
to sullen inertia,
her face a lachrymose mask,
heavy with the lacklustre listlessness of - straw.

Yes we did, yes we did!..
The two of us, is right!..

Oh, many's the card was dealt
from the bottom of the deck!..
You, me - us!..
'Hard, we were hard - oh, very -
often, too often - on that wee one!

'So many ways!
In so many lousy, selfish, coldly uncaring ways!..

Promise - and then not deliver...

Say back at such and such a time - then not show...

Leave her at night, asleep, hoping she wouldn't wake
before we got back - stinting on a baby sitter...

Leave her in the car while we slipped in for a quick one...

'Keep her in a pub - smoke, noise, adult voices
getting louder by the round -
when we could have given her space, clean air,
the dignity of a quiet home...

Lavish her with sweets while robbing her of security...

Buy her toys - a swing - then confuse her
with sudden swings of mood, changes of humour...

Buy her a bike, then piss off in the banger...

Charge her with responsibility - then charge out...

Cast her in a part years before she was up to it.

Leave her schooling to Sister, her spelling to Sesame Street.

Put her down, scold, dismiss her - when we should have
buoyed her up with praise, encouragement...

Yes, we did. Oh, yes we did...
Our deadly sins... of omission...

'Getting back now, the neighbours...
from the pub, the meeting, the night-out - whatever...
Driving slowly... keeping themselves to themselves...
Careful not to ask after her, mention her name...
They know. That's how I know they know...

Hello, yeah?.. Ah, Patricia...

Eh, not so bad... And yourself?..

A do? How do y'mean?.. Barbeque!..

Well, I hope you get the weather you're expecting...

Ah, very kind of you... but, look, Pat, I won't promise...

Well, to be honest, I - Ah, now you're twisting my arm...

How do y'mean, someone?

God, but you're gone very mysterious all of a sudden...

Well, I... Can we leave it open, just for the minute,

let me sleep on it?..

Ah, you're an awful woman...

All right, but I'm warning you:

I'll be going round like snuff at a wake...

Oh, and I won't be staying long, that's telling you straight...

I suppose himself will have the apron on?.. Ha. I can

imagine... You, too...

Good luck a while... and thanks for the...

'See you, Pat... 'Bye...

Saturday, huh... Any time after nine... Hmmm...
Won't hang about...
'Not easy, nursing a coffee... coke...
while the rest of them are letting it back.

'Wants me to meet someone, huh?..
I could nearly see her smiling on the phone...
Up to her old game, Pat, in-introducing people...
setting the ball rolling... making and matching.

Maybe a young one, bursting out of a tight skirt,
eyes glowing, finding me pale and interesting...
longing for the companionship of a mature,
protective male?..

Ha. An ould maid, more likely...
Ah, sure who'd have me?..
Still, you never know...
Someone, maybe, who'd take me on... over...
organise me?..
'Set out to be all Emma never was -
and never could be...

Another missile on the way? Direct hit?..

'Turnip in the goolies?.. Or a carrot?..

Or mebbe just a, a high-velocity pea?..

So watch it, huh? Head down, me ould flower.

There's a thing about women:

they have more ways than one

of bringing the tears to a man's eyes...

JENNY ONE, TWO, THREE...

*Hello, yes?.. Jenny! God, would you believe?! Just this
minute I was - Listen, how are you?.. Ah, that's great,
I'm delighted... Good, good, that's my girl...*

*And how do you find the new job?.. 'That early?! So
who calls you for God's sake? The trouble I had –
every morning!.. An, an alarm clock in a... in a basin?..
What are you trying to do, wake the landlady as well?..*

How, how do y'mean, not there any more?.. No, that, that's all right. Just... you might have told me. Yeah, just a sec... I have a pen here, some - Okay, fire away. Four seven eight... yeah... one three three... Ah ha. And where's that?.. What!.. God, but you're a long way from Trafalgar Square!..

Jenny?.. Jenny, are you okay?.. No, come on, I can hear it in your voice...There is, there is something... 'Course. You don't have to ask me that, girl. God knows, you know me well enough by now... Anything... You can tell me any...

Hmmm... Yeah... And you?.. I see.

No, no I'm still here... Just thinking, that's all... Oh, I knew you were gone on him... Well, to be honest, I was hoping it would fizzle out... Like, I know he doesn't kick with the right foot... I, just put it down to you, your in-insecurity - needing someone - bit of support - in the Big Smoke...

No, no I'm not hurt... Okay, it's okay... If... like if you had told me, I mebbe could have gone over... to be with you... meet him... even make a few days of it...

In a...? Oh-hh... I see...

No, look, we'll leave it at that for now, okay?.. No, no that's all right... It's just, it'll take a wee while to sink in... this end...Okay?.. Okay...

Ah, I'm surviving, still above ground... Well, you'll write to me, eh?.. 'fill me in - your new address... Oh and here, hey! You tell him from me, if he's not good to you, I, I'll go over there and, and burst him!.. You, you already have?!. Ah, sure, you're way ahead of me...

'Course I do. Always will... 'Member, remember - years ago - you used to look up at me and say, Only the two of us, Dadsers?.. 'Sure, you do... Mind how you go, girl...

'Bye... Bye, Jenny.

There y'are, that's more of it... Just when you think you're back on your feet, steady, keeping the head down – whammm!.. Like a ton of bricks...

Hmmm... In a Registry Office... Huh... My daughter... in a... Well... thank Christ for small mercies: if it goes sour... 'years to come... she'll have an out... be able to get off the hook... won't be nailed to a cross... have to go through what I, I...

And we haven't even met. Him. Me. 'Don't even know what he looks like, how he sounds. All I know is, he - he's into my wee one... I, I'd rather not think about that...

'Some class of a maintenance engineer, so she tells me - whatever that means. Be God, if he doesn't maintain her I, I'll - !..

No. No, I won't. In-interfere... She's on her own now... 'paddle her own canoe...

Did she - have to?.. 'Didn't say... Ah, hardly. A doctor over there would have her on the pill in jig time... Still, you never... 'Know soon enough, I suppose... 'Hope not, for her sake... 'Give her a chance to get her bearings before, 'fore she has to batten down the hatches, surrender to the, the finality of family...

I should be hopping mad. Livid. Furious...

How dare she!.. Let us down - me, herself!.. 'Hitch up with some quick-talking gobshite!.. No permission, blessing... No ceremony, sacrament, binding in Heaven...

All that... Huh. If they paid me, I couldn't muster a spark this minute... Just dead inside, that's all. Dead... God knows, we all do mad things when we're young. Sure who am I to talk?!.

And I suppose, looking back, it was on the cards that she'd head off, in at the deep end, find out the hard way, take a few knocks...

But Jesus! Jesus Jenny! To go and - !..

London, huh... The Enveloper... 'Only Adoption
Society known to many's an Irish lad and lassie.

She'll put down roots now... Family in suburbia - or
wherever... Weens spouting the Queen's English -
clipping vowels, mincing consonants - in pace with the
tempo of the great Get-Up-and-Go... Knowing little -
caring even less – about a rich heritage this side of the
sea...

God, but she was a gorgeous child!
Pig tails flying in the wind,
freckles framing a ha'penny nose,
hop-hop-hopscotching
outside our front window,
safe on a tarmacadam road,
secure in a quiet cul-de-sac
in snug suburbia...

And growing up she was out on her own,
head and shoulders above the...

Here... I have it here... some -
Ah-hh!.. First Communion photo...

Jenny looking out from 'neath a veil:
open-eyed... trusting... distrusting,
unaware of what was out there,
what lay ahead... in the world beyond
home and hearth and convent school...

All she knew that morning was that white
was for purity, innocence,
that Jesus was coming to her,
really and truly present
in the Sacrament of the Altar.
A wafer on her tongue, distilling,
within her, Love, Peace, Serenity...
a stillness of mind and body.

'Knew, besides, that later there would be
congratulations, celebrations,
nicies and goodies and silver
in her rosary purse...

How's this it went?..

"You have given yourself to me,
now let me give myself to Thee...
I give Thee my body that it may be
chaste and pure... "

And by her side, so proud of her,
parents she was justly proud of:
Hairdo… outfit... suit... tie.

"In a bit closer… look at the camera...
Now smile, big smile... Ah, that's it!.."

Golden day of golden days...
before the storm clouds gathered
and the rancour of marital strife
rent the domestic fabric.

'Seems like yesterday she was going to bed with her
dolls... And the toy horses on her locker coming to life -
large as life - cantering, ever so gracefully, round and
around her room, lulling her, in slow motion, to heavy-
lidded sleep...

'Night I walked the floor with her... there and back, there and back... cradling her in my arms... her whimpering... head on my shoulder...

Unbearable, unbelievable pain... searing earache...

Sssshhh. There, there, a leanna...

Waiting for a doctor - any doctor - to call, diagnose, prescribe, leave free medication, pharmaceutical sample... depart, fee-paid.

Only the two of us, huh?.. Dad. Dadsers... Not any more. Just me now. Me and the four walls. Not even the dog for company... Traffic, huh. How he came by the name, I'll never know...

Oul' ejiit. Looking up at me, ears arched, eyes quizzing, tail motioning in apprehension, wondering what sort of mood I was in, what to expect: a pat on the head or a kick in the arse, left in - or put out for the night..?

I didn't tell her. Jenny. Hadn't the heart. Enough shocks for one night... A letter?.. Yes, yes that would be... 'Explain, on paper, how he eased gradually downhill... slowing, going blind...

The Vet and back, the Vet and back... That last night I stayed up into the wee hours, him shivering, sickening, shaking... on the bed I had made up in front of the fire here in the lounge... until he... 'till he... Traffic.

She'll die when she hears... God, but she loved that mongrol... 'Used to talk to him. And he to her. Sometimes. I think... Chemistry. Vibes. All that... Bit weird, if you ask me...

But then, her mother used to talk to the cats - before they got fed up waiting for a bit to eat and fecked off with themselves...

Could you blame her?.. Jenny. Talking to the dog... 'Bout the only company she had, betimes... Well, her mother was forever coming and going: in one door, out the other...

And sure half the time I wasn't here - off chasing one story or another... Or pinned down in town, filing copy for the early edition... And even when I was, I wasn't - all here... Not all -

'Getting home of an evening after a session on a high stool to do my famous imitation of a father: hurrying upstairs - Ooooppss! - for a tuck-in hug and kiss... a stab at a night prayer, a go at a bedtime story...

Don't, don't forget to say your prayers, Jenny...
Always... No matter how - how you're feelin'... Even a,
an ejaculation - lot better than nothin'... 'Safact...

"As I lay down my head to sleep
I pray to God my soul to keep...
Is he in Heaven or is he in Hell,
that damned elusive - "

Oh, no! That's not how it goes... Sorry. Sorry, love.
'Teaching you the wrong one.

Sorry, Lord. 'Went off the rails there for a minute. A bit... 'Get it right. Tomorrow night. 'Make a fresh start... To- tomorrow... 'Nother day...

What?! Tell, tell you a story? Ah-hhh... Look, it's getting late, Jenny, and you have to be up in the... Hmmm... Well, it'll have to be a quick one - I, I'm very...

All right, then... Okay. Just the one, mind... Here we go: Once upon a time... a very, very long time ago... there was an old, old...

God, when I think of it! Looking back... This little girl, holding my hand, clinging to me... waiting, wanting - oh, longing! - to be moulded.

And I, I paid her scant attention. 'Thinking, ages before she... years and years yet agrowing... Plenty of time to, to... More fool me.

Oh, I tried. Now and then, here and there, to be a, a parent... 'real dad... just like the other men in the Estate.

Like the day I took her to the pool...

That's it, that's the girl... Push with your legs... Hands cupped, under your chin... Now sweep out, out with your arms... Push, push with your legs... Now glide... Easy, nice and... Yes! That's it!

See, you can swim! Ah, that's my Jenny...

Hmmm?.. 'Deep end?.. Well... all right, then... Just hold on to me, okay? I won't let you...

Here we go, now... Easy, easy does it... All right?..

Ooooopps!.. Okay, okay, I have you!.. It's all right, all right, Jenny... Just a slip, that's all...

No, of course... 'course I won't let go of you...

I played it down. But yes, yeah... 'No denying... she got a fright. We stayed with it, though, stayed in there until her, her fear of the deep began to abate...

Dad! Hold me, Dad!..

Oh, Jenny, Jenny... I held on to you, girl, as long as... And when the time came it was you that let go of me, flew the nest. Ah, but sure, that's the way of it - and that was years ago...

We went back the following week, and the following... A few swims after that it, it just seemed to fizzle out... Me. My fault... 'Didn't get back in time... or, or there was something else on... or I, I just lost interest... to be honest...

Honest? Huh. Honest...

We wish you a merry Christmas!.. We wish you a merry Christmas!.. And a happy...

Did I? Really?.. Wish you a Merry Christmas, Jenny? That Winter?.. Y'know, like - warm, cosy, nice-to-be-here, never-to-be-forgotten?..

Presents and cards and crackers... lights on a real tree by the window in the front room... And telly, telly! Wondrous entertainment in glorious colour!..

Lots of chocolate for me to eat,
Lots of coal making...

Oh, a spoonful of sugar helps the medicine go down... the medicine... go down... go down...

Christmas Eve... I got it right - for once. The shopping, the fuel, the decorations... All that day I was the model father – whatever about an ideal husband...

And no booze. 'Not as much as wet the lips... Later on - oh, well before the shops shut - I sallied forth one last time... 'Special, oh a very special assignment: to buy Jenny's very own present...

What was it to be?.. We'll see, we'll see...

Hey, there's my local and look, look at the cars outside! Some of my best buddies in there, the cream of the club... 'Bet the craic is only ninty... Just the one?.. A quickie?.. Come on, pull over... Indicate, turn the wheel - or did it turn by itself?..

Damnit, you won't be seeing them for the next few days and if the weather turns foul..? One beer, wish them all the best, and you're on your way... Still plenty of time to buy the book, the game, the tricycle - whatever... Ease into second... unto a high stool...

Well, will you look who's here?.. If it isn't himself!.. We were only talking about you this minute... Here, come're - what are y'havin'?..

The first pint went down like velvet... the second was mother's milk... and when I stood up to go, car keys in hand, someone had sent me over a double, compliments of the Season...

I slumped... feet nailed to the floor... Cru-crucified... Gluepot. Bloody gluepot.... I was still there coming up to closing...

Frost on the ground... windscreen. Put her on pilot... slow home. Ease in the door... Schhhhh... Not a sound... Them asleep above... Empty... empty-handed...

She'd wake in the morning - *"Hurray! It's Christmas!"* - and hurry downstairs in nightie and slippers and dressing gown and high excitement to the lounge, the Christmas tree and - nothing...

Nothing but the heavy snoring from the master bedroom en-suite.

Oh, you bastard! You contemptible shithead!

Incredibly, she forgave me... in time. Oh, indeed...
'Only remains for me to, to forgive myself... Maybe…
some day...

Now… what did I do with..? Ah, yes - this, this one…
Oh, there were other letters, yeah, sure... But they, they
were just letters... y'know, the usual... what she
reckoned I'd like to hear… shadow boxing... But this,
this one was...

*Dear Dad... I want very much to tell you how I feel
about US, to ask you to try to see things from my point
of view. Please bear with me, Dad, I don't have the gift
of words like you; so I may wander from the point and
get a bit confused from time to time, but as I said, if you
could just bear with me...*

I loved my room at the top of the house, Dad. You gave it to me when we first moved in and I loved it. It really was "mine." My room... I used to look out the attic window a lot, not just to have a smoke - but to look around me.

At the mountains on a clear day, at other houses, at the sky, or maybe at the massive tree in the next back garden...

It seemed to me that tree changed the colour of its leaves every few weeks. And though I loved the way it shone a blaze of reds and coppers and browns and yellows in the Autumn, I used to watch for the green to appear so I could believe in Summer.

Sorry, I seem to have wandered already...

Dad, you never encouraged me to watch TV and I never really felt comfortable being downstairs. So I would bring my coffee and biscuits back up to my room and shut the door and get on with it.

I'd turn on a tape and sing, or I would take out some paper and paint or I would read or write letters, and

occasionally I did some study... And downstairs didn't
belong in my room.

So you could be in the foulest of moods and it ceased to
matter, anymore, when I was up there. You had your
golf and your pub pals and your newspapers and the
television programmes you wanted to watch - mostly
the news and the weather forecast...

I had my room and it was up there I made up my mind
to leave. So that I could just do what I wanted, when
and how I wanted, and the only person I had to justify it
to was myself and God.

Dad, I used to wish sometimes that you would leave me
be. I wish that you could have said to me, Have a good
time when I was skulking out. Or asked me if I had
written any good poems lately or whatever...

I just wished that when we sat down and talked it
wasn't only for you to tell me to study, to stay in, to
take down my posters...

You decided when we could talk and it always had to be a major event after the News. You didn't want to know about aspects of my life that to you seemed trivial but were to me very important.

I know you want only the best for me, want me to be happy, lead a healthy and productive life. I know that before you ever give out advice, you really think it through from every angle so as to give me the maximum of your wisdom.

And, like you are, Dad, it wasn't easy to sit back and let go a little, give me a bit of slack.

And although when I left home you wouldn't speak to me for ages and that hurt - hurt, hurt! - I wouldn't let on for a minute that it did. But I wouldn't wish it on anybody. The fears, the uncertainties...

And even now, after all this time, when things are going badly and I'm feeling down, the only place on this earth I want to be is at home, in my room, and you there to say to me that everything will be all right.

But what makes me swallow my fears and keep going is knowing that at long last you are proud of me and at the end of the day that's worth more than gold dust.

Now you and I are friends, Dad, great friends. We can just talk normally to one another and I adore it. I love you completely, Dad. Sometimes when we have been speaking on the 'phone or I get a letter from you, I could just burst with the love I have for you.

Dad, you are a great father, you really are. But I have to tell you, when Mum took off, it ripped the heart out of me, it really did. It was easy, in a way, to keep it to myself, it was that deep. One of my teachers used to say my face was a mask. How right she was.

And I know you were hurt, too, hurt terribly, though you tried the best you could, not to show it, to me, anyhow, maybe me above all. And I know it wasn't easy for you, bringing me up on your own, especially when I got older, got out of hand.

And for all our rows and falling-outs, I loved you, Dad,
loved you the sun, moon and stars. Don't ask me to
explain, I couldn't. It's what I feel, not what I know...

I'll post this now, spelling mistakes and all! If it helps
clear the air, fair enough. If not, at least I can say - I
gave it my best shot, Dad! And that's something else
you taught me... I love you, Dad. Love you to bits. And
always will. No matter what. Jenny.

Hmmm... Follow that, huh?.. *"Love you to bits, Dad."*
And she does, I do believe she does. Deep down...

Even loves, betimes, my very inadequacy,
hopelessness. Like the day she glanced up at me,
frowning, from the Pets' Column in the evening paper
to ask -

Dad, what's a rough collie? I mean, why is it called rough?. .

I hadn't a clue...

Eh-hhh... Well, like... y'know... the way they go – 'Ruff! Ruff!'

The look on her face! Incredulity quickly giving way to irrepressible mirth...

Ah, years ago, now. The doctor passed me on
to a specialist and he said –

"We'll have you as good as new in jig time..."

Oh, nothing major. Still, a general anasthetic is a -
well, it is!

I checked into an inner city hospital:
Gaunt, red-bricked, Victorian.
Creaking all the way from Main Entrance
to X Ray, Reception to Theatre,
Canteen to Cardiology...

A Men's Ward that seemed to stretch forever
across a sea of russet linoleum
to Dickensian lavatories.
Floor polish and disinfectant.
Harassed nurses, whirling past,
fighting fatigue, resolute in white.

The old and the not-so-old:
empty-eyed, withdrawn, distressed.
Smokers coughing abominable sputum.
The cameraderie of an optimistic few:
wheezing gems of wisdom -
honed bons mots - in pristine Dublinese.

And then it happened,
the January of the Deep Freeze:
storm winds beating against the windows,
snow swirling down, blanketing,
from an ink sky...

Next day, stand-still:

impassable roads, treacherous footpaths.

Yet she made it. Jenny. In to see me.

Lurching, slipping, swaying, falling...

'Determined to reach me on the eve

of the Big Knife.

I glanced up from a so-so paperback

to find her at the end of my bed:

smiling, glowing, radiant,

melting snow on anorak and headgear,

exuberant at the challenge of it all...

Jenny?... But how - ? No, I mean...

Oh-hh... Ah, come here to me... Oh, Jenny!

Jenny a leana!

Oh, Dad! Dad, will you be all right?

God, Dad, if anything happened to you I,

I don't know what I'd... I'd be lost.

No, Dad, nothing must happen! You're to

come home to us, safe and well, have to!

Mum sends all her love and says she'll be in to see you as soon as...

She'll ring in the morning, first thing, to find out how - how...

Dad, I'm using all your tissues...

And Traffic says - I thought of this on the way in - to give you a big Ruff, Ruff!

Some, some things you just can't forget...

So much I could have done for her: forming, leading, strengthening, moulding... helping her to... nurturing the sapling...

Try. Again?.. Do, yes... Reach out to her... Only this time, follow through, make it stick...

Jenny?.. Jenny, 'tell you what:
why don't we go together on Sunday,
say to the eleven Mass -
how about that?..

How d'you mean, cool?..

So... At week's end I would clean the slate... descend
on some unfortunate priest. Ha. He won't know what
hit him! And if he's nodding off when I step in, well...

Back row, centre aisle.
A tangible stillness in an almost empty Church...

Elders moving slowly -
genuflecting, kneeling, standing -
making their way to Calvary,
treading their very own,
plaster statued, Via Dolorosa...
re-living the Greatest Story Ever Told
in reparation for their own sins
and the sins of the world.

Jesus is condemned... the weeping women...
Falls the second time... Veil of Veronica...
Nailed to the Cross... Company of thieves...
Sitio, I thirst... Sponge of vinegar...
This day you will be with me in Paradise.

Stopping, betimes, to nod, whisper, chin-chin -
in-house salutations, parochial palaver -
silhouetted against flickering candles,
framed by altar lights,
passing by the stray soul nursing
a luke-warm radiator.

Pausing to petition the Sacred Heart,
Our Lady of the Miraculous Medal,
Saint Anthony, the Little Flower:
'grace of final perseverance,
'grace of a happy death...
and so to the Beatific Vision.

Clink clank of copper and silver into Offerings Box:
for the maintenance of the Sanctuary... the new roof...
the Foreign Missions... the poor that are always with us.

But where the crowds, the queues,

the thronging congregations of Yesteryear?

Singing out with one voice a hymn to Mary?

Whatever happened to Saturday night?..

Red glow over drawn curtains of

Confessional: invitation to reconciliation...

Should I..? Will I?..

Ah, do. Do in the name o' God.

Open the door, step in,

kneel by a walled Crucifix,

whisper through a grill, darkly,

when the slide is drawn back...

Yes, but how am I going to tell him all?

And will he shoot me down, bawl me out?..

In this day and age? Hardly...

Bless me, Father, for I have sinned...
It's a good while now since my last...
Well, I stayed away because...
I, I'm married, Father, and then again, I'm not -
if, if you know what I mean...
She, she went away... 'Someone else...

Since then I, I've had a go at the Commandments -
all ten...
Yes, you could say that: some more than others...

Eh, just the one. She'll be twelve in another wee while...
Oh, no, she's with me - except the odd weekend...
Ah, the best I can... 'Not easy. To be honest with you,
I'm not much of a parent, even at the best of times.
And at the worst I, I can be a holy terror.

Well, like, coming the heavy... Or letting her down...
Raising my voice - maybe even giving the odd roar -
when things don't go to my liking. Or I, I'm a bit under
the weather... It's that more than anything...

I mean, if there's a sin at all on my soul I'd like lifted,
it's the way I go on at times with my young one...
So I, I'd just like to make the peace with Himself...
I will, Father. I'll try again...

He gave me the Rosary. The Sorrowful Mysteries.
'Commended me to Our Lady. I'm never to forget
that Salvation came to us through a woman... Ha.

Sorry. 'Sorry, Lord. I, I'll try... Again? Again...
God. Getting up, falling down... The Agony in the...
Dark in Gethsemani. Or was there a full moon?
Between ominous clouds, gathering?..

Chalice...
I beg, beg you - take it away. Still, not my will...

Our Father who art in Heaven... Thy will be done...
in the Garden... at the Praetorium... on the Cross...
Forgive us our trespasses... as we forgive those...
as I, I forgive… forgive… her. Wife.

There, I've said it. And I'll try -
try the best I can -
to, to mean it...
Turn the other cheek, eh?
Take it, full force, in the face, to the jaw.

Tilt. Incline head in submissive anticipation
of another shock to the system...

There y'are. That's Christianity for you. Difficult?
It's just about bloodywell impossible!..

Lead us not into... deliver us from... evil. Evil.
Deliver me, Lord. Please deliver me from - myself.
Free me from this, this wallowing in the past.
Spare me the torture of riveting recall...

Hail Mary, full of... Blessed art thou amongst...

Are you there - or are you on your travels?
Above - or beyond in Yugoslavia?
I, I'm never too sure when I have you,
to be honest. But then, you're a female.
So I don't find it all that surprising...

My mother was always there and me growing up.
When I got home from school or in off the streets
or back from the pictures or after a football match
or, or if I was in a fight with some other gang,
she was there. Always seemed to be - there.
'Can't remember a time she wasn't...

Remember, o most gracious Virgin Mary...
To thee do I come... before thee I stand...

There was this shrine, as I recall.
Oh, well known it was, locally...
We walked the three miles, there and back.
Out the country. 'Summer's day...
Me still in short trousers,
'boots that needed mending.
Six miles in all. A killer...

'Knelt for the Rosary. Nudging, gawking around,
stifling a giggle... Every bead a penance...
Grass trodden underfoot by previous pilgrims.
The tree and the hollow, the rock and the glade,
the stream where we filled our bottles to carry home.

Our salute to you wafting out on the warm, still air:
Calling to pray... In sweet tones announcing... Ave... Ave...
The Lourdes statue marking the ledge
where you appeared... whenever it was,
to whoever it was... reputedly.

We had you to ourselves in those days -
before you took off on a world tour...

Holy Mary, Mother of God...
And mine. My mother. Are you? Really? Hmmm...
Well, I'll tell you, straight up: they're not all like you.
Women. Some of them can be right - ah, well, no.
I won't say it out. 'Too much respect for you.

'That anyone who fled to thy protection...
was left unaided...

You came through it all, fairly well, so they tell me.
And now you're on a direct line to Himself -
easy access, unlimited credit,
excellent equity, buoyant stock -
in-interceding for us...

All I'm asking is that you put in a good word for me -
hoping you'll understand, even if He doesn't -
so that when the time comes
I won't be caught on the wrong foot...

And look, I know you're inundated
with all sorts of prayers and petitions.
But I'd ask you - as a special favour -
to look out for my wee one.

She's heading for the rapids and there's
nothing I can do about it...

Well, you only have to go as far as
the porch if you don't believe me!
Out there in the street: teenagers
on their way to the Pub, Disco, Rave -
paying scant attention to this
granite structure, dim-lit Presbytery...

And in no time at all my wee one
will be one of them:
on-stream, 'full spate...
in tow, keeping up...
matching their form...
cool, laid-back, with-it...
Maybe even a leader.
In thrall to her peer group.

So please, will you keep an eye on my Jenny?
God knows, she could do with a bit of mothering.
And why not? Ah, now! 'No better woman...
Do. Oh, please. Put your mantle about my daughter
and protect - save her.

Oh, I know, there's the nuns and they're doing
their best, I'm sure, and they're an extension
of your own good self on earth, doubtless.

But they seem to have their hands full
and they stream, unmercifully,
and if you don't mind me saying so,
their idea of Instruction, Christian Doctrine,
is a far cry from the Penny Catechism...

Oh, Mother of the Word Incarnate...
in thy clemency graciously hear...

'Years ago, my wee one,
holding my hand, looking up at me:
'Only the two of us, Dadsers!..
To tell you the truth, we're both a bit
lost in our different ways..

Oh, oh. Sacristan swishing down the aisle,
keys a jangle, signaling close-down...
poised to see off the last of the faithful few.

Return to house, flat, home, family...
to another, to others, to no one...

The tea or the cocoa,

the fire and the hearth,

sober survival...

Multi-channel viewing,

wide choice of alternative worlds:

Moscow to Washington, Belfast to Belgrade,

The Gaza Strip to ER, Crime Watch to Iraq,

Match of the Day to the Late Late,

National Geographic to the Movie Premier...

God, I'm hopeless! 'Can't even get through

a Hail Mary without going off the rails...

I thought, mebbe, Jenny and me going to Mass together

would bring us closer... help her - me - to stay on the

right track, stick to the straight and narrow...

Ah, but it didn't last. As she grew older there was the

pull of her peer group, strong as the swell of the sea...

'Happened under my very eyes. Oh, I knew it was on the way, but still... One day she was there, at my side, leaning on me. The next - almost without my noticing - she had grown up and out and away...

How was her childhood? Brief... How now her girlhood? Over.

Just, it seemed, as I was beginning to get the hang of Jenny Two, she disappeared, almost without trace. Enter from far right, Jenny Three.

My offspring had changed - quietly, irrevocably, almost surreptitiously... And I, sad to say, changed towards her.

Will you have some of this?.. Huh... 'Not hungry...

Sure how could you be hungry? 'Always stuffin' yourself: sweets and biscuits, chocolate and crisps – and you're a hoor for hulahoops...

Gung and gunge... Is it any wonder you have pimples?
And you'll look marvellous with a brace – oh, a sight
for sore eyes!.. 'Tired talking to you... But you won't
listen, will you?..

The next thing I know you'll be on the fags. And then
it'll be the hard stuff... And if you go at that the way you
let back orange and coke, you'll be hooked in no time...

The genes, do y'see, there's no reckoning with the
genes. How the Hell would I know what's inside you?
'Chances are, you're a sitting duck... Ha. Will you look
at you!.. Sitting duck is right...

My teenage daughter: 'Wearing all that weird gear...
Black. Gothic. That thing stuck in her nose. And bloody
big boots the farmers threw out years ago. 'Face like
whitewash... Be God, there'd be more colour on a
monkey's arse!

Ah-hh... Let her off... let her off!

Lipstick and eye-liner and perfume, rings and bangles
and jewellery, men's shirts, waistcoats, pyjamas...

Fellas and dates and discos, posters and mirrors and blow-driers...

Endless phone calls, ages in the bathroom, beguiling manipulation, terrible, terrible tantrums, and a deafening sound from the stereo...

God, give me patience!.. Help me to hold myself together is all I ask, Sweet Jesus!..

I loved my room at the top of the house, Dad. You gave it to me when we first moved in and I loved it. It really was 'mine.' My room...

Hmmm... She told me in all honesty before she took off that she had done a thorough job, left it tidy... Tidy? Tidy! It took me the best part of a week to clear and clean, get it into some kind of order... Now it's tidy. Now. Tidy and - empty...

How many times - dear God, how many times! - did I ask her to pick things up... not to stuff drawers... cram

presses?.. How? How many times?.. A waste-paper
basket was a game: hit-or-miss.

Larger-than-life posters spanning a slanting ceiling:
David Bowie... Guns 'n' Roses...

Oh, I got them down - but they didn't give up without a
struggle: flakes of paint, strips of wall paper, on
varnished floor boards... scatter rugs that hadn't had a
brush or a vacuum for many's the long day...

Prints, photos, post cards, snap shots... glaring graffiti...
cartoons of doubtful pedigree... Blue tac and cellotape,
paste and glue, clips and nails and drawing pins...
Markers and crayons and chalk... Mounds of dust and
fluff atop the wardrobe...

Cigarette papers, spent matches, in a tin under the bed.
Mascara on the duvet, lipstick on the pillow case... A
wasted stylus in the damaged arm of the record player...
Wads of chewing gum under the student desk.. A
lifeless bulb in the reading lamp meant to help her
focus on -

I'd turn on a tape and sing, or I'd take out some paper and paint or I'd read or write letters... And sometimes I did some study...

Sometimes?.. Sometimes!.. Well, as long as you didn't overdo it!.. That wasn't the deal, kiddo... You were up here to keep the head down - for the most part, anyhow. 'Not moon in a mirror, gawk out the window, arse around...

Sure I knew the time would come when you'd want to fly the nest. Sure I did...

But I wanted so much you to have something going for you - so you wouldn't be going to nothing... The freedom you craved was right here, within these four walls... here - on the shelves of this bookcase...

On and off the course... Texts you dallied with but never really tried to master...'Would have been the makings of you, set you free. In a way. Maybe the only way that really counts, in the long run...

Dad... Dad, you never encouraged me to watch television -

That's right, I didn't. Didn't! 'Switched it off, more often than not - to facilitate you, inconvenience me!.. I did it for you, can't you see that? The box was the enemy, destroyer of concentration, application!

So I would go back up to my room and shut the door and downstairs didn't belong in my room. And you could be in the foulest of moods and it ceased to matter, anymore... And it was up there I made up my mind to leave.

When she took off I gave her a month,
'month at the outside...
She'll be back, nothing surer.
Head hanging, glad to be home, safe shelter.
Oh yeah, London'll cure her cough...

Oh, Jenny, Jenny!..
What are you at, a tall a tall, daughter mine?..
I didn't give you a hope - how could I?..

Learning the hard way...
Getting by on an apple and a Mars bar,
skimping on this, going without that,
maybe borrowing, on pay day, your fare to work.
You were lucky you didn't end up in a
cardboard box on an arctic side-street...

'Scratching and scraping at the bottom
of the barrel...
trying to get a foot on the first rung
of an endless ladder.

Answering one small ad after another
after another... hoping for an interview -
chance, a chance, yet another chance -
to lie and bluff and bluster your way
into a no-hope job -
a number in a menial menagerie,
a cog on an insignificant wheel -
praying that this time - this time! -
you wouldn't be caught, tripped up, checked out...

But the weeks passed. And the seasons...

She hung in there, held out, roughing it.

No way would she give in. Pride?.. But of course.

And a strong resolve to stand and give challenge.

But kept in touch - the occasional letter, phone call.

Dad, I have to tell you, when you and Mum broke up it ripped the heart out of me, it really did...

All right, all right... 'Point taken. You were disturbed, right?.. 'Think you were the only one? Do you?.. 'Lots of kids, lots of broken homes, this day and age... Your friend, Breda, did all right for herself, right? 'Father died when she was a ween and her mother an alco, off the wall...

Shane across the road from us survived - and he had to contend with breakdown, split... a rented house in town... a new and officious mother... Right? All right?!

No, it wasn't all right, Dad!.. It wasn't Breda or Shane or Margaret - it was me. Me! And if they coped, fine, great. But I didn't - couldn't... We were all together, Dad, in those First Communion photos - check it out in the Family Album...

Ah, yeah... sure, go ahead... blame me... For every bloody thing... Leave me wondering was it me, my fault... all my fault?.. Mea maxima culpa…

Hard... Hmmm?.. Jenny?.. There's a hardness there now... Huh! Is it any wonder?..

But for all our rows and falling-outs, I loved you, Dad, loved you the sun, moon and stars... Don't ask me to explain, I couldn't...

Sometimes, on a clear day... moonlit night... I climb up here and open the ceiling window. 'Look out and across Dublin Bay... to London... so far away...

And even now, after all this time, when things are going badly and I'm feeling down, the only place on this earth I want to be is in my room, at home, and you there, Dad, to say to me that everything will be all right...

Here… this top landing… witnessed many's the row and many's the making up…

Y'know, I believed her - oh, for ages! - when she told me this, witnessed to that… 'Took a long time for the penny to drop.

And then it was quite by chance…
when I stumbled across,
checked out,
came upon,
uncovered an incontestable scenario to the contrary…
Only then it began to dawn on me:
my darling daughter was a
seasoned,
addictive,
compulsive
purveyor of blatant fictions…
Liar! 'Bloody liar!..

Dad. Dad, you're stronger than me. Bigger. And you can shout louder… Please. Will you swap places, please, just for a minute? You be me… down here… looking… looking up… up at you… you when you're in a foul humour…

There, on your face, it's there - the anger, frustration,
turmoil... threat of explosion... And I ask you, would you lie
were you me - to escape the wrath of Hell brimming over?
You would. 'Course you would. To be sure. To be
comparatively... secure...

And a thief into the bargain!.. Took, snitched, lifted, helped
herself to anything that took her fancy without as much as by
your leave or would it be all right if..? My socks...
cigarettes... deodorant... tennis racket... videos...

The loose change I was wont to leave on the mantlepiece.
The dinner jacket I seldom wear and didn't miss for ages -
smuggled out and given, on loan, to a girl friend from down
the way...

Was anything sacrosanct? I was never one for after-shave
and when I put it to her that the bottle was almost empty she
took it in her stride, glowed reassuringly, and gushed -

Ah, look, Dad! You didn't screw the top back on, properly - it
evaporated...

'Made her way through the house from top to bottom.., examined the contents of every drawer... recorded, in precise detail, the location of every single item: a graphic inventory that would stay with her wherever she went, however long her sojourn...

'Knew every crook and cranny... 'Could identify - and step over - every creaking floor board... slipping out, sneaking back in...

'Not good enough... just not good enough!

But when I confronted her she reared up, bluffed, brazened, swore black and blue... pitching her voice against mine... higher and higher still... Lie upon lousy lie...

'Sank further and further
into a quagmire of irrelevant
protestations, non sequiturs,
a morass of pretentious,
preposterous bullshit.

Oh, she knew - knew full well -
even as she looked me in the eye
that I knew that she knew
she was lying.

Then sudden deflection - a lightening transfer of guilt that
would have left a three-card-trick man gasping...

Only after I had faced her
with undeniable evidence,
irrefutable proof -
and only after she had simmered down, cooled off, re-
grouped -
did she finally admit to me,
here, here at the top of the stairs -
a sort of confessional
under the skylight -
that yes, she had, had indeed...
Tears and sobbing voice,
whispering admission.

Oh-hh-hh... Knife edge at my heart.
What to say?.. What to do?..

I fear for you, girl, I really do...
If you go away from here
to live and work among strangers...
get caught out in a lie...
caught with your hand in the till...
there'll be no absolution,
paternal admonition,
on the carpeted steps
by the bannisters...

Dear Dad, This could be so simple for me to write, I could just scribble down some poetic touching thought, but I still wouldn't have expressed my true feelings. So this letter is going to be plain and to the point, but it's so hard to get down on paper.

Dad, I can't start listing off all the things I did wrong before I left home. We both know how wrong I was and now I am sorry. More than anything I would like to talk to you, to sort this mess out, to tell you from my heart how sorry I am, how much I really love you and miss you, as my Dad.

Please take this letter as being sincere. I need you, Dad, in my life. Please don't block me out. I know I pushed you away, or rather I ran away from you. One thing I will always regret is that I never put my pride aside and asked for your advice on my plans, or indeed advice on anything... I love you, Dad... I'm so sorry...

But does she?.. Mean it?.. This time?.. This time mean it?.. Or is it more of the same: baiting... hooking... reeling in the slack... playing me for a cod?..

I've grown up, Dad. You'll see. Grown up at long last.

I can't wait... 'Easy to be palsey wallsey when you're a few hundred miles apart.

I'll be home for Christmas, Dad, for sure... like always. Wild horses wouldn't stop me!..

'Sleep all day, stay out all night...

But this time I'll be home to be home - if you know what I mean. Oh, look up a few old friends, sure, but I'll be around that much you'll think you're being haunted!..

And I'll make the stuffing and cook the dinner.
And I'll decide what programmes we watch, okay?
Okay. That's cool...

For Christmas... a fortnight in Summer... Bank holiday
weekend, if I fork out the fare... But not to stay. Never again
to put down roots.

Too many restrictions, Dad. Too many do's and don'ts. For
all your central heating, fire in the front room, it's still a cold
house...

I'll wash and stack, you dry and put away, okay? And if you
take your coffee up to the 'phone you bring the mug back
down to the kitchen, right?.. And if you don't use a saucer
you'll leave a ring mark on the hall table...

And look, you're still only sixteen: if you go out at night I
expect you back at a reasonable hour... Oh, it's an old saying
but a true one: show me your company and I'll tell you who
you are...

Dear Dad, I want you to know that I still say my prayers and go to Mass on Sunday. Well, not every Sunday, to be honest. But nearly every... See, I won't tell you a lie. That day's over. And if I do miss Mass I say a few extra prayers during the week. Especially the one you taught me - the Serenity Prayer.

... to accept the things I cannot change... courage to change the things I can... and wisdom to know the difference...

And I still have that card you gave me when I was leaving - FOOTPRINTS. It's up on the wall over my bed, place of honour... And sometimes I think that's me walking along the sea shore, side by side with Jesus. Two sets of foot prints...

And after a while I look back and see only one set... And I turn to Jesus and say - "Why did you leave me, Lord, when I most needed you?" And Jesus answers -

I didn't leave you, Jenny... When the going got really tough, I carried you.

And Dad, Dad! I've started going out with someone. His name is Jason and he's really, really nice...

Jason... Jaysus, Jason.

One of the most considerate, loving people I have ever met. We started out as friends and I swore that's how it would stay, but both of us have admitted defeat and we are nearly sure it's love. We have talked about it many times, because it could easily have been infatuation...

First time I met your Mother I looked into her eyes - and I was gone.

I think it's special this time because he keeps telling me not to be running myself down all the time, to think good of myself, to aim high... I have never had such respect from a man...

Funny you should mention infatuation...

He has given up cigarettes, never drinks or does drugs, so I always feel safe around him. I'm not saying he's goody goody, he has his faults like everyone else, and the beauty of it is that we both see each other's faults as well as the good things.

Couldn't see... just couldn't see ahead...

In two months he has taught me to relax around people, that I don't have to pretend or to try and prove anything to anyone. Most of all, he has taught me to be true to myself and therefore I am true to others.

What do you know when you're young?.. About anything, really?

So I won't pretend to you, Dad. He is not a Catholic and for the life of him he cannot understand why Catholics and Protestants in the North are killing each other...

But he is really, really Christian and I honestly believe that's what counts in the long run... Would you agree with me there, Dad? I know Mum would...

Oh, yeah. Sure she would. As long as it didn't mean an early rise, sackcloth and ashes…

But Dad, what makes me swallow my fears and keep going is knowing that at long last you are proud of me and at the end of the day that's worth more than gold dust.

Now you and I are friends, Dad, great friends. We can just talk normally to one another and I adore it. I love you completely, Dad. Sometimes when we have been speaking on the phone or I get a letter from you, I could just burst with the love I have for you.

'Came the day I booked a flight,
packed an overnight bag,
made a phone call, headed for Heathrow,
London Central...
I wanted to see my daughter, that's the why!

- Jenny! Jenny, over here!

- Dad! Oh, it's great to see you, Dad!

- God, you look -

- How are you? -

- Wait a minute! Who's saying what to who?!

- All right, then, we'll start again, okay?

- Okay.

- Now… let me look at you... Hmmm...

- What, Dad, what?..

*- Well... For one thing, you're too thin in the face
and too much on the hips...*

- Dad!?

*- You've been eating all the wrong food,
I know, I can tell...*

- Ah, Dad...

- For another... I can't take my eyes off you!

- Oh, Dad, that is so-oooo! -

Jenny, my Jenny!..

We walked and talked -
bumping, laughing, nodding, skirting, glancing,
taking each other's measure -
until we came to a restaurant off a main street
that looked just the job...

How do you like your spaghetti, kiddo? Al dente?..

To be honest, she was far more interested
in the homemade ice cream smothered
in chocolate sauce!

Over coffee she fished a camera
from a God Almighty hold-all -
and a passing waiter duly obliged.

Just you and me, Dadsers!..

And when she excused herself to go to the loo,
I knew she was having a quick drag.
But not in front of her old man.
Not yet. Not quite yet...

'Came the time to finish, settle, tip -
Grazie, tanta grazie! -
exit into the crisp night air,
the emptying streets… the Underground.

'Have to leg it, Dad!

I to my hotel, she to her burrow in outer suburbia.
Down and down again... cavernous... dim lights...
echoing footsteps... eerie, outer-space noises...
We waited, platforming with the other,
gathering, late-nighters...

Will you be all right, Dad? You know where to
change? Write, won't you? Big long letter. You have
no idea how much it means to -

I stepped into an empty carriage,
turned, and our eyes met:

Oh, but I do, I do... I'll ring you, Jenny. Soon as I -

No! The doors edged shut and it was moving,
gathering sudden speed...
Jenny static, riveted,
eyes brimming, limp hand waving -
Then she was gone... I was gone.

The doors opened again at the next station...
In a way, they had closed for good.

And so much gone unsaid.
So much beyond and below the chatter,
chit chat, small talk…
A hundred - oh, a thousand - things
left unspoken, unshared... I to her, she to me.

Still only a child in ways, wee girl, my Jenny...

I, I left something of myself on that platform.
Behind, on that platform. And even if I wanted it back -
But I wouldn't - wouldn't ever want it back.

God go with you, Jenny... I can't...

Yes. Yes, that's the way of it... No holding on.
Let her be... chart her own course… into deep water.

'Had it framed. The print she sent me.

'Not a great 'photo, not much of a camera, but still...

Here, on the mantlepiece... by the clock.

When I light the fire of a winter's evening,

switch on the occasional lights,

it seems to catch the glow...

Jenny. Jenny Three and me...

arm in arm in Il Corvo -

a chocolate-sauce-over-ice-cream

ristorante...

God, but she was a gorgeous child... I can just see her!..

Pig tails flying in the wind, freckles framing a ha'penny nose as she hop-hop-hop scotched with the other children, safe on a tarmacadam road, secure in a quiet cul-de-sac in snug suburbia...

I eased into second gear, swung round the corner, pulled up
at our semi…

I was getting out, reaching for jacket and brief case, when
she sighted me… A squeal of delight and she was dashing
forward, eyes dancing, face radiant, knowing I would turn to
meet and greet her, sweep her up and into my arms, shower
her with –

Suddenly she tripped, pitched, sprawled.
A stricken silence - then the pain, shock, sobbing
embarrassment...

Oh, Daddy... Daddy!

I hurried forward... lifted, carried her indoors… the other
kids turning away, nodding in silent sympathy…

*There, there. Hush, love, hush. Sssshhhhh... Show me: oh,
dear, dear... Your poor palms and your knee, bleeding...
Come on, now, come on... Ssshhh, wee one, ssshhh... Sure,
we'll have you right as rain in no time... I'll sponge away the
grit and grime and there's plasters in the kitchen press where
we keep the cough bottle and the linament...*

No, no it won't hurt. I would never hurt you, don't you know that?.. No, nor let anyone else hurt you... My girl, aren't you?..

You got a fright, that's what it is... Hmmm?.. What's that?.. Tripped? No, no you didn't trip, Jenny. No, the road jumped up and hit you, that's what happened...

Bold. Bold road... There now, 'see?.. You're smiling, again...

Yeah! And, and laughing!.. Jenny... Jenny One... Wee wet Blue Eyes...

Eh-hhhhh... What did I do with that number?.. 'Give her a quick call... Ah, yes - here... What's the time?.. Oh-hh... 'Chance it... 'Won't let it ring for... 'Might get an answering machine... Now... anyway... 'Soon see...

Hello? Hello, is that - ?.. God, don't tell me I have a wrong number?.. 'Jenny not there, Jenny Byrne?..

Oh? Oh-hh!.. No please, please don't! Hold
on, no, no don't wake her, please! It's okay.
'Not, not urgent... It's just - she rang me
earlier and I...

'Didn't realise it was so... Did - did I wake
you, too?.. Ah, thanks be to...

So... You must be - Jasper?.. Sorry, Jason!..
Yes, of course.

Jesus, I'm hopeless with names, always was!..
Jason. Now I have you... Ah-hh... Ah ha...

Yes, yes she did. I mean, I know - know the
story... So.

I'm to con-congratulate you, wish you every,
you both every... Oh well, there y'are, that's
the way... You win some, you... I, I've lost a
daughter and gained a - ha, ha - a bathroom...

Sorry. Sorry, son. I, when I'm a bit jumpy I'm
inclined to act the maggot... No, no, maggot...
MAG-GOT... What?.. Ah, forget it, 'doesn't...

Oh, yeah... Yes, well yes... 'Love to. Now that we, we've broken the ice... Indeed. I, I have a few days due to me... London'd be as good as any... Right... Get together, smooth out a few...

Ah no, no need. Save yourselves the call. You'll have to watch every penny from now on... I'll ring again in a few days...

Well... we'll leave it at that. For now... 'Good, good talking to you, too... All right, then.

Oh, and look, tell her - when you see her in the morning... tell her... just say, I... I love her to bits... no matter what... and always will... Will, will you remember that?..

All right, then... Good night... Night, Jason...

God bless...

THE END.

29330523R00151

Printed in Great Britain
by Amazon